Minotaur Revisited

by David Gelber

Ruffian Press
150 FM 1959
Houston, TX 77034
www.ruffianpress.com

Library of Congress Catalog Number: 2012918180

ISBN-13: 978-0-9820763-7-8
ISBN-10: 0982076371

First Edition – 2012

Cover Design:
Duncan Long
www.duncanlong.com

Typesetting/Book Layout Design:
Gianna Perada
www.brighteyes.org

Printed in the United States of America.

Minotaur Revisited

by David Gelber

RUFFIAN PRESS

Dedication

Minotaur Revisited is dedicated to everyone who has ever felt they were different, who did not fit in, or who believed that they didn't matter. I hope that The Minotaur's amazing life will make you realize that even the most unusual individual is important and can make a difference in this crazy world.

1.

THE PRESIDENT OF THE UNIVERSITY stood before the multitude that packed the auditorium, a crowd composed of students, professors, politicians, religious leaders, and visiting dignitaries.

"Ladies and gentleman, I present to you, 'The Minotaur,' the half-bull half-man resident of the Labyrinth of Crete, beast of myth and legend."

A well-dressed being approached the podium. He was over six feet tall with the body of a man and the head, neck, and shoulders of a bull. Fingering the lapel of his perfectly-tailored black suit, his fingers were neatly manicured with a gold band on the left fourth finger and a gold watch on his left wrist. His polished and pointed horns sparkled from the stage as he began speak:

Let me just say from the start that the majority of the writing and artistic depictions of me have been utter lies; fabrications woven by jealous and envious individuals who cannot believe that someone who is different from the norm can be anything but a monster.

I mean, look at me; does the sight of me make you want to run and hide? I admit I'm different, but aren't we all different outwardly? It's really what's inside that counts. At least that's what people say, all those clichés that do nothing but irritate me: "Beauty is only skin deep; beauty is in the eye of the beholder; it's what's in your heart that counts," and on and on.

Let me tell you up front that I did not choose to look this way. My odd appearance is purely an accident of birth. One is never allowed to choose one's parents, and in my case, my exact parentage can only be called, at best, murky.

It seems my mother, Pasiphae, times being what they were, was not averse to sharing her affections with any willing person. She was not what one would call "discriminating," even though she was married to the king. And King Minos, from what I was told, was more concerned with affairs of state, than affairs of the heart. It seems that over the course of a week or so, Pasiphae shared her affections with no less than twenty different suitors and she did her best to bestow favor on each. One of them was somewhat "bullish" in his affections, at least that is how she described his advances.

Perhaps, my unusual appearance is a joke played by the gods. Perhaps the particular suitor who fathered me *was* one of the gods. Or maybe I'm simply a genetic freak, a mutant. I do know for a fact that she did not mate with the famed white "Cretan Bull," that particular story being part of the myth that surrounds me. Of course, the origin of my unique physique (how clever, that rhymes) is of no consequence. I am what I am, to quote Popeye, and that's all that I am. I'm Quinton, the Minotaur Man. In actuality, my name is Quinton Arbus Taurus Aegus Minos, but please, just call me the Minotaur; the name commands respect.

At least far more than "Quint."

I was lucky my mother was the Queen. If I had been born of the common folk, no doubt, I would have been cast into the sea to drown; it seems that a mother's love had some limitations in those days. However, being a prince, of sorts, I was safe. My mother treated me as every mother should; she protected me, kept me safe, guarding me and threatening any would-be assailant with summary execution should they attempt to harm me in any way. She did her best to educate me, but she herself was not the brightest star in the sky. Still, she was my mother and I wouldn't be talking to you today except for her.

However, even a queen has restrictions to her influence. Minos saw me as a means to establish political order and maintain his power throughout the ancient world. When I was twelve, he built the Labyrinth and shut me inside. It was quite an elaborate maze, really. Its sides were nearly twenty feet high and were composed of dense shrubbery barbed with razor sharp thorns. The only escape was to find one's way through the complex maze and, trust me, this was a daunting task. I was in there for years and I never found my way. And believe me, I searched and studied endlessly. I tried to mark my trail, but there was something about those bushes that made fruitless any and all attempts to escape.

All I could do was wait. I wasn't completely idle, however; I tended a garden in the middle of that enormous maze, growing figs, dates, olives, and grapes. A colony of bees settled nearby and every autumn treated me to combs of very fine honey.

The stories accusing me of devouring young maidens and feckless youths are pure lies. Surely, you are aware that we bovines are strictly vegetarian. I know what you're thinking; I'm at least partly human, but you can surely surmise that I am not such a barbarian as to be a cannibal? Those young people were delivered into the Labyrinth; that much is true, but I rarely saw any other human. They usually died of exposure and malnutrition, being lost for days and weeks among the endless twists and turns. Once in a while I would encounter a young lad or maid and would do my best to help, but they would flee in fright, and more than once they were flayed open by the razor-sharp spines that grew on that accursed hedge. Thus, my reputation was born. I was the feared Minotaur who devoured his victims every nine years. And what did I do all the rest of the time? Sit in the center of the Labyrinth, howl at the moon, and do Soduko? Give me a break; I'm not a beast, you know. These stories acted as propaganda spread by Minos to maintain control of his conquered territories. The implied threat, that the fierce Minotaur would be released and wreak havoc on the helpless inhabitants of the ancient world, was all Minos needed to maintain his power. And it would have continued for years if it hadn't been for that scoundrel, Theseus.

2.

THESEUS. THE HERO OF ANCIENT mythology.
My supposed slayer. Yeah, right.

Mythology, that's an understatement. Oh, sure he was sent into the Labyrinth to be devoured by the mean old Minotaur, but the actual events have little to do with the myth that surrounds him. I am living proof that he never assassinated the fierce Minotaur. Here's what really happened:

Theseus came with the usual group of so-called sacrifices from Athens to serve as my dinner. While waiting to have his sentence executed, Ariadne, the king's daughter, got the hots for our less-than-noble hero. She fixed it so that he could find his way out by giving him a special ball of thread and also instructions as to where I could be found. Of course, he didn't really have a sword hidden in his tunic. The guards weren't that stupid. He bribed one of the guards to leave a sword inside. And Theseus really was a buffoon. He didn't care about that girl, but, being the pig that he was, he still was willing to use her and seduce her for his own lust, but I'm getting ahead of myself.

Theseus made his way to the center where I wasn't sleeping. I heard him coming an hour before he arrived. Anyway, he came at me as if to fight, lunged at me with his sword and fell flat on his face and passed out. The great hero was stone cold drunk. I sat by him and poured cold water on his head until he sobered up and, when he started to rouse, I picked the poor lad up by his hair and gave the meanest snarl and growl I could. Well, this "great hero" immediately passed out again, but not before he vomited all over me. I threw him to the ground in disgust and was about to walk away when he finally spoke.

"I can help you, Minotaur," he cried. "I can give you what you want, even more than you want or could wish for. Just help me out a bit."

"What could you possibly have that I could want, you sniveling, cowardly excuse for a man?" I answered, but I did stop to listen.

"Your freedom, if you play your cards right."

This certainly piqued my interest, but I was also wary. How could this drunken, lowlife excuse for a man get me out that place? I thought about fulfilling the legend, just once; you know, bump him off. I figured the world would be a better place without him. Still, the possibility of getting away intrigued me. Zeus knows I didn't want to spend the rest of my life tending fruit in the middle of a Labyrinth. So, we hatched a plan.

I let loose with wild howls and screeches and scratched my arm with his sword. I smeared my blood on his arm, tunic, and sword, and then I gave him a horn I had shed, definitive proof of his conquest. He strapped the prize to his tunic and left, promising to leave the path of thread in place so I could follow him out at nightfall. Still, I didn't trust him.

Night fell and I proceeded to follow the white thread to freedom. I promised him I'd leave Crete immediately, so as not to interfere with the "great man's" plans for power. As I followed the thread in the dark I was careful to leave the trail intact, just in case. Halfway out, my worst fear came to pass: the path disappeared. Theseus, I'm sure, figured I'd be stuck, either have to go back or die, lost in the maze like so many others. But, I wasn't as stupid as he thought.

I'd filled my old horn with some dust, dust with special properties, dust that glowed in the moonlight. Having been trapped inside that Labyrinth all those years, I'd become a student of astronomy and I knew there was supposed to be a bright full moon that night. Just as planned, the full moon emerged from behind a cloud and, like magic, the path before me became clear. It wasn't a revelation from above or anything in the least bit mystical; it was the carelessness of Theseus. The dust that had trickled silently from the horn glowed in the moonlight. Theseus, as I'd anticipated, had pulled on the fine thread before he exited, assuming that this would obscure the escape route. But, the path lay plainly before me and, with a bit of care, I found my way closer to the exit.

I was making pretty good headway when the moon went behind the clouds and the path started to fade. I followed as far as I could, but a short time later I was stuck in the dark. Then to make matters worse, there was a crack of thunder, a flash of lightning, and a torrential downpour started. It lasted only about ten minutes, after which the full moon returned, but the path was no longer visible, washed away like the "itsy bitsy spider." Now I really was stuck.

"Think… think," I said aloud. "Maybe I'm close to the exit." I closed my eyes and sniffed the night air. The salty scent of the sea filled my nostrils and I followed my nose to the exit, which was only a few twists and turns away. Before long I was free.

I should have simply left, made a clean getaway, and gone on with whatever life had in store, but I couldn't resist a bit of fun sprinkled with revenge. I followed that drunken fool, Theseus, in my own ship, followed him and his smitten maid to the island of Naxos. She was prostrate at his feet, about to surrender herself to that lowly rascal, when I burst out of the surrounding bushes and confronted the double-crossing loser.

"You have the audacity to pretend to love this woman, you cheating, lying scum," I growled. "Tell her. Tell her your plan; tell her about every other unsuspecting maiden you've had your way with, how you use them and throw them away like the pit of an olive. Tell her."

I had him about the throat and the look of terror in his eyes as he felt my hot breath on his neck was all the revenge I needed. But I'd underestimated his charm and overestimated his "innocent" prey. Instead of the indignation, anger, and remorse I'd expected, when Adriane learned the truth about Theseus, that little wench stood at his side; fearless, she got between us and pushed me away.

"Get lost, you big ape, this is my affair; I know what I'm doing!" she screamed, standing on her tip toes, her face only inches from mine.

"I'm not going to spend my life as handmaiden to that wretched old Minos," she continued screaming, poking her finger into my chest. "I'm here to have a bit of fun and maybe I'll end up Queen of Athens, but you had to stick your pointy-headed nostrils into my affairs. Butt out, you freak. I can take care of myself."

The sight was surely comical; diminutive little girl staring down the fierce Minotaur and, truly, at the time, I almost burst out laughing. Of course, having the head of a bull has its benefits. I'm sure neither one of them recognized the big smile on my face. I'm sure they thought my expression to be more of a defiant sneer. Anyway, I left them to themselves. Theseus got what he deserved. Years later, I learned that he *had* abandoned her on that island and she had cursed him and tragedy followed. These facts are accurately reported in the current mythology. Personally, I don't blame him for leaving her, just as I'm sure that Minos breathed a sigh of relief when he learned she'd left with Theseus.

But, enough of those two. I left them to their ways and headed west, making my way to Egypt, where I was greeted with a most unexpected reception.

3.

MY VOYAGE TO EGYPT BEGAN smoothly enough. I was able to purchase passage on a Phoenician vessel with little fuss and no questions. I trimmed my horns and kept my head covered; those Phoenicians, they'd sell their own mother if the price was right. They left me alone during the trip and I stayed to myself. There was a little dog aboard who kept coming up to me, sniffing my cloak, and yapping all the time. His name was Ramen, like the noodles. One day out from Egypt there was a big storm, which blew the ship close to shore and then dashed it against some underwater boulders, throwing all of us into the sea. I managed to stay afloat, quite a trick considering how big my head is, and who do you think climbed on my shoulder for a free ride? That little mutt, Ramen.

I was, surprisingly, a pretty strong swimmer and after another day I made it to the Egyptian shore. It must have been quite a sight as the two of us emerged from the surf. I remember the early morning sun was behind me as I climbed out of a huge wave breaking over the sand. I had seen the crowd of people on the beach and decided to add a bit of drama to my arrival. I crawled out on all fours first and then slowly rose up, accenting my silhouette against the illuminating sun. I'm sure I presented an imposing figure. I added a few growls for effect and the people certainly were startled and then overwhelmed.

As I walked on the sand they fell prostrate in front of me, their faces buried in the sand. I was declared, "Nev, God of the Surf." Luckily, I spoke fluent Egyptian, a byproduct of all that time locked away in the Labyrinth, and was able to address the adoring masses.

"I come to you from the waves of the sea; my father bids you welcome."

"NEV, NEV, NEV!" they screamed, running up to me, kissing my feet, and placing wreathes of flowers around my thick neck.

Having nothing better planned, I accepted their accolades and worship and started on one of the happier times of my life. Ramen tagged along and I actually grew quite fond of that little dog.

I was carried to the city of Luxor, borne by six bearers on a magnificent throne. I was given a splendid palace where I lived with Ramen, attended by a cadre of priests. The palace was lavish, filled with every convenience and embellishment of the day: polished stone floors, gilded fixtures, a continuous stream of water flowing through my quarters, servants of every size and shape catering to my every whim; a true paradise.

I was months in that wonderful palace before there were any visitors or demands of any type. Each day was filled with beautiful young girls attending to my every need. Parades of exotic beasts performed solely for my entertainment. There were sumptuous banquets and nightly visits from willing young and apparently fearless maids wishing to mingle with a god. I must say I enjoyed myself. I told myself I deserved, compensation for the years pent up in that cruel, impenetrable maze.

Each day, I arose mid-morning to be bathed and pampered by my devoted staff. My horns were polished, my hair styled, sometimes in the most ridiculous manner, but I didn't care. Breakfast followed, then some sort of show: acrobats, juggling bears, dancing girls, anything that my people thought was fit to entertain a god. I tried my hand at painting and sculpture—with some success, I must say. I took to drawing images of Ramen, who faithfully stayed at my side.

This loyal little dog certainly was an excellent judge of character. Any visitor that drew a growl from my canine friend was dismissed. After a while, those who came with requests must have either learned (or were told) to bring a treat for my furry companion because after a few months, Ramen rarely rejected anyone.

Being a god, I was expected to have extraordinary powers, wisdom, and discernment. My afternoons were often filled with sorry individuals who came for counsel, blessing, or judgment. I did my best, but I wasn't very experienced in the ways of the world. Nevertheless, these petitioners hung on my every word, and I suppose I managed to accomplish something worthwhile.

It was an idyllic life, but, like so many things that involve humanity, it couldn't last. Egypt was ruled by Pharaoh, Thutmose by name, and he considered himself to be a god. Unlike me, he truly believed it. His wrath boiled against me and he plotted to bring me down. He came to see me, ostensibly to seek counsel on the important issues of the day, but his questions were more to feel me out, to probe for weakness or signs that I was not divine. His transparent motives did little to impede his inquiry. After all, if his investigation proved me to be merely mortal, to have all the needs of men, then he would also be indicting himself. He truly *was* mortal, he needed to eat, sleep, love, and everything else, and he would eventually die. Although I didn't know it at the time, I was not so encumbered. As you can see, I am still here, thousands of years later. Whatever the accident of my birth, I have been blessed (or cursed) with unnatural longevity.

Pharaoh's plots took on several forms: poisoned food, devious servants, and finally, attack by his finest soldiers. All were repelled, shrugged off as trifling nuisances, which, of course, only increased Thutmose's anger. I suppose these troubles would have continued if it hadn't been for Moses' appearance in Pharaoh's palace. Because, whereas I was a mere annoyance, Moses threatened to upset the entire economic order of that nation. Moses came to free the Israelites, former guests turned into slaves. It was a great battle of wills: Pharaoh, the great Egyptian king who considered himself to be God vs. Moses, the messenger of the, alleged, one true God. I have to say the things I saw were truly amazing.

I wasn't "in the front row" for this battle of wills, but I certainly saw the results. Here's the set up: Moses, apparently a Jew, had been raised in the palace and Pharaoh was acquainted with him. Forced to leave Egypt under duress, Moses married, had children, and settled into an agrarian life miles away. Later, he was called to return to Egypt and foster the release of the Israelites from enslavement to the Egyptians.

The battle that ensued did not involve spears or chariots, but only the forceful will of these two individuals. The plagues came, an annoyance for me, but calamity for Pharaoh and the Egyptians. The final plague, the Angel of Death called down to smite the first born of Egypt, was more than Pharaoh or his people could endure, and the Israelites were to be released. Lucky for me, I was second born in my family, so I was spared the power and wrath of the Israelite God. With great fanfare, whooping, shouting, and celebrating; with bags overflowing with the spoils of a battle they never fought; the Israelites left. Talk about trash talking; if they had left with even a touch of humility, none of the subsequent troubles would have transpired. But, they had to stick it to Pharaoh, deepen his humiliation, and anger him even more. I don't know why their God chose these people. Moses was okay and one of his lieutenants, Joshua, was a very noble, level-headed individual. But the rest? I wouldn't give two cents for the lot of them.

The whole drama was far too fascinating to ignore and as the Israelites left, I followed discreetly from a safe distance. I told my servants that it was time for me to return to my dwelling place—the surf—and I made my exit, leaving behind everything but what I could carry. (Ramen had settled down with a lady hound and chose to stay behind.) It was easy to follow that mass of humanity, hundreds of thousands of men, women, children, and animals moving slowly into the barren wilderness, supposedly trusting in their God to bring them to a land of salvation. They got there, all right, but the journey was, shall we say, complicated. Being a mutant beast, I chose to follow at a safe distance, worried that my startling appearance could cause an unexpected reaction.

The exodus was a study in organized chaos. At the front was Moses, staff in hand, following his God into the blistering, cruel desert, with only his faith to support him and thousands of people looking to him for hope and guidance. I can only imagine the burden he felt: one misstep and it would be the end. It seems that the economic upheaval weighed far more heavily on Pharaoh than the loss of Egypt's first born. After a time, he sent his chariots to return his wayward slaves. Some say it was out of compassion, fearing that the Israelites were destined to perish in the desert following a deranged, misguided leader (the official government statement at the time). The soldiers were to return the Israelites to Egyptian "protection," and any that resisted were to be abandoned in the desert without provision.

Everyone knows the story of the Israelites reaching the shore of the Red Sea, how Pharaoh and his soldiers trapped them against the waves and were then held at bay by a pillar of fire. But the story behind the scenes in Pharaoh's camp has never been told. You see, at this point, I was behind Pharaoh, also restrained by the Israelite's God. However, I was up on a hill and clearly saw the parting of the Red Sea and Moses leading his people between the roaring walls of water. Once they reached the far side, Pharaoh hesitated to send his men after them. So I gave him a little nudge. Noting his uncertainty, I came up behind his chariot.

"Some great king you are," I scoffed. "Are you so afraid of your former slaves and their God?"

He turned and flashed his dark eyes, which moments before had been full of fear. "I have no fear of you or the worthless Israelites," he shouted and spat on the ground.

"But you hesitate, Pharaoh. You're afraid to reclaim what belongs to you. You refuse to avenge your first born. Look at me; I'm Nev, the god of the surf. I will hold the sea at bay, even if the Israelite God does not."

He looked at me, still with doubt in his eyes.

"Do you hear the laughter, Mighty Pharaoh? The sound travels quickly across the sea, doesn't it? You have my word of honor: You and your men will be safe." I stood as tall as I could. "NOW GO!" I shouted.

The pillar of fire was gone and he turned to his captain, "You have your orders. Bring them back or destroy them." He turned to me and said, "I'm trusting in you, great Nev, protect my people."

"All that is in my power I give to you, Mighty King," I lied, trying hard not to burst out laughing.

As the soldiers started down the banks and charged between the walls of water I made a quick getaway. I was pretty far away when I heard the roar and crash as, just as I expected, the sea closed in on the soldiers and their horses. I actually felt sorry for those men, sent to their death by that foolish king. I was also sorry that Pharaoh had not accompanied them. Still, after this fiasco Thutmose's days as ruler were numbered. It was only a few months later that he was found with his throat slashed, allowing a new, and perhaps, more accomplished man to ascend the throne. He did manage to do one thing before his untimely end. He wiped out every trace of my ever having set foot in Egypt. If you look at the archaeological findings from Egypt, tracing back to those times, you will find evidence of a variety of gods: Ra, Isis, and many others, but no Nev, which is a pity, because for a short time I was the only god they truly could say was real.

As for me, I crossed the sea in the more traditional manner, by boat, and eventually caught up with the Israelites at Mount Sinai where there were some new, peculiar things happening.

4.

I SAW THE ISRAELITE CAMP in the distance. Actually, I saw clouds and lightning, and heard thunder; the source of the disturbance was something on the top of Mt. Sinai. As I came closer to the camp there were a few men stationed on a flat plateau, while below a throng of people milled about. Occasionally one or two would glance up at the mountain, then walk away quickly, shaking their heads. At first I stayed hidden. An atmosphere of tension and worry permeated that place and, needless to say, I didn't want to cause more unrest by suddenly appearing. I feared that my unusual appearance would spark a riot and riots have an unpredictability factor that can become particularly unhealthy, if you get my meaning.

I stayed and watched, however, sensing that something big was brewing high up on that mountain. The clouds and thunder and lightning went on for days; the fear and worry and grumbling increased until I heard shouts from the camp.

"Moses must be dead; no man could live so long in the middle of all that raging, unceasing violence. If we stay here, surely we will die. God has forgotten us; we've been brought to this place to die."

So little faith, I thought as I continued to watch and listen.

"We need a new god, one that we can see, one that we can touch, not the empty air that Moses gives us."

I listened even more closely and I guess I was careless.

As I shifted, some dirt and rocks fell from my hidden perch. Almost as one, the frightened band turned to me and started to climb towards my hiding place.

Not much choice, I surmised as I stood up. The fearsome sight caused the Israelites to pause and then (I was starting to get used to this) they bowed down. Silence gripped the camp and, like the wind blowing through a field of grass, they kneeled to me.

"Here is our god! The answer to our prayers, a real god that we can worship!" someone shouted. "Let us make an image of him, to pay homage to this true deliverer."

I wasn't sure what to say, and I was a bit worried. After all, I'd seen what the Israelite God did to those who tried to cross Him. I decided I needed to set the record straight.

"Israelites, I am no god. Your God dwells on this mountain; you must have faith."

Shouts rose from the unruly mob. "You're our god! You will save us! Save us... SAVE US... SAVE US!"

I tried my best to dissuade them, but a fearful angry mob is a dangerous thing. I stayed where I was while they went to work, building an image of me out of gold. I have to say, it was a poor likeness; more of a calf than a bull. As they finished, after the requisite bowing down and pledges of allegiance, the sense of fear vanished and the ceremony degenerated into a huge orgy. After a while, they forced me to leave the relative safety of my elevated sanctuary and mingle among the masses. Big mistake.

The throng of Israelites was drunk on wine and on the freedom that comes from a crowd that has been stripped of all inhibitions. Some of the things I saw made me blush; however, before long I had joined them. They set me up high above the crowd, brought me wine and food as well as young women and men. They brought a particularly attractive young maiden and tied her to a stake before me, stripped her naked, and prepared to plunge a knife into her heart, a sacrifice to their new, as yet untested god. As they were about to plunge the sharp blade into her chest a shout came from above.

"YOU WICKED FOOLS! YOU HAVE SINNED A GREAT SIN!" His voice became a bit softer. "I have spent all these days on this holy mountain receiving God's Law, written by the fire of His own hand. You are not worthy to receive it. You set this creature above the only true God. Now, receive His holy word."

He held the two stone tablets above his head and threw them down, hitting my elevated chair, causing it to explode into flame. Bolts of lightning followed and the earth started to shake and rumble. Some tried to climb to Moses; a few clung to me; I tried to escape, pushing and kicking the mass of people away and jumping from my perch just before a flash of lightning struck.

All around me men, women, and children were being swallowed up by the earth as wide chasms opened up amidst bolts of lightning and rumbling of thunder and earthquakes. I thought I'd escaped as I lumbered away, but, stupid me, I had to stop and look back at the carnage. At that moment there was a loud crack and, all of a sudden, I was standing on air. I fell straight down and came to rest, with a loud thud, on a ledge about fifteen feet from the surface. I held on for dear life as the rumbling continued. Luckily there was a cleft in the sheer wall that I could cling to. Almost as quickly as the upheaval began it was over. I looked up to see sunlight peering in through the gap above my head as I surveyed my predicament. The irregular ledge was about eighteen inches wide, the walls were sheer stone, except for my tenuous handhold, and below me was black nothingness.

This is a bit of a pickle. Serves me right for trying to play god, I thought.

"OK, God, I got the message, no more pretending to be anything other than a monstrous freak. You win," I yelled out loud.

No answer; not even a grunt or a belch. *Back in the Labyrinth.* I waited and waited and waited. Day became night became day became night and still I waited; waited for a miracle. What happened next wasn't exactly a miracle.

Or, perhaps it was.

5.

I T STARTED DURING THE NIGHT after I'd been trapped in my prison for about three days. I heard a howl-ing from above, the wind I presumed. With the sunrise I could see sand blowing above and some of it blew down into the bottomless pit that was my jail. *Just great, sand filling the air; I won't be able to breathe.*

But, I could breathe and the wind kept howling, the sand kept coming and the bottomless pit turned out not to be so bottomless. Sand filled that deep hole and when it was level with my ledge I gingerly stepped off. I started to sink and, for a moment, I thought I was going to be engulfed, but I was able to put my arms out just enough to support myself and over the next few hours I inched my way out. As soon as I crawled out, the wind and the sand stopped.

"Somebody's looking after me," I said aloud as I surveyed the land. The mountain was quiet now and all traces of the Israelites were gone, swept away or buried beneath the sand. I didn't know where they had gone and I had no idea where I was going. All I knew was that I was tired of people. So far, my few encounters with "normal" humans revealed to me that the supposed "best of humanity" wasn't very good. The-seus, Pharaoh, the Israelites all shared two things: selfishness and depravity. *Time to get away for a while.* I looked up at the sun now rising in the sky. Turning to the right would take me to the sea and back to Crete. Heading opposite the sun would return me to Egypt—not a very pleasant thought, towards unknown territory. I took out an Egyptian coin and tossed it in the air, Jackals I go left, hieroglyphics I go towards the sun. The coin landed on the ground and buried in the sand, with the edge sticking up; no luck. I looked around a bit more. To the left was downhill. I took my chances and headed in that direction, South, I realize now, towards central Africa.

It wasn't very pleasant, trudging through the sand and battling wind and sun. I really don't know how I survived, except that I discovered that I was very durable. I could go a long time without food or water and I didn't tire very easily. I walked and walked, always heading south. The terrain changed, sand gave way to grass, and grass gave way to trees. I eventually found myself deep in the jungle, surrounded by huge green trees, birds with bright plumage, snakes, and all sorts of animals—monkeys, leopards, the occasional lion, hippopotamuses, elephants—in short, every type of African animal you'd see on a Sunday morning showing of Tarzan the Ape Man. Only there wasn't any Tarzan, no Jane, no Boy, no people of any sort, at least not that I could see. I did hear the occasional drum, but I didn't see a human for years. I was actually happy to be rid of them.

Still, I hadn't completely lost my sense of civilization, at least not yet. I went to work building a home of sorts, up in the trees, away from the numerous slimy beasts that crept and crawled on the ground. It was a most remarkable tree house, with a ladder fashioned out of the trunk of the tree and a rudimentary bed and chair. Over the years the area became a bit more refined, even as my need for the usual sort of comforts faded away. I made friends with some of the birds, amazing parrots that could make sounds that closely mimicked lions and hippos and other birds. An orphaned baby leopard moved in for a time, until he grew too big and seemed to be eyeing me as his next dinner. Later on, another furry little creature moved in and made itself at home, apparently adopting me and acting like it was doing me a big favor, allowing me to live in the house that I'd built.

There was plenty of food available for the picking, water was only a few steps away and humanity, at least for the first few years was noticeably and, gratefully, absent. The clothes I'd worn gradually wore out and I went about naked, not that any of the other animals cared. Once again, I was happy; content to live this life of solitude, away from fear, ridicule, and worship.

But it had to end. I'd heard distant drums off and on since the beginning, but as time passed, they started to move closer while still well away from me. The people of the jungle lived a nomadic life and I began seeing lone men venturing into my end of the jungle, usually brandishing spears and knives—hunters, no doubt. They did a poor job of camouflaging and it was easy to hide before they found me. I figured they'd move on through and then it would be back to my life of solitude. Instead, they settled in. These people were a bit different from the Egyptians or Hellenists I'd come in contact with in the past. They had almost pure black skin, were very muscular, and also went about naked. They had a language of sorts, which was completely unintelligible to me (of course), but, otherwise they seemed just as other humans I'd known. The men hunted and acted tough while the women ran the show. It took about a year, but they finally moved on.

After they'd packed up and left, I went through their old village. As I walked among the broken frames of houses and piles of human refuse, I heard a whimper. That's when I found her, Alena, which means pretty; because she was the most beautiful little girl I'd ever seen. As I went up to her, she didn't move, she didn't cry, she wasn't scared, and I soon learned why my appearance didn't startle her and why she'd been left behind. It was apparent that this lovely child was blind and in that cruel, jungle world any sort of weakness spelled doom.

I wasn't sure what to do with her, I mean she was only about two years old and what did I know about children. *She's better off dead*, went through my head, but she smiled and then, I guess she sensed that I was standing nearby, so she stood up and came towards me. She said something, words that were incomprehensible to me and then she hugged my leg. Well, my heart melted at that point and I scooped her up into my arms and hugged her close to my chest. We'd both been rejected by humanity and now all we had was each other.

She quickly learned to cling to the bullish part of my neck, which made for fairly easy traveling through the jungle. She wasn't, I guess the term now would be "potty trained," which made for a few accidents, but she learned quickly (and I also learned quickly) so that after a few weeks this was not a problem. She was able to eat most anything and she thrived on coconuts and fruit, which was our main diet, and she grew. She graduated from clinging to my neck to riding piggyback and she gave up her native tongue and learned Greek.

She learned her way around my tree house and for the longest time we were ecstatically happy together. Her disability was no more than a slight nuisance, while her laughter filled my life with joy. The world was perfect; she was perfect. I did my best to teach her all that I had learned, about nature, the sun and wind and rain, which food was good to eat, what animals were dangerous, and everything else that was stored in my head. She was more than an apt pupil, even with her lack of sight. She could discern plants by their feel and scent, knew which birds were which after only a brief touch and a few peeps or warbles. In short, she was amazing.

I still worried about her, though, and rarely let her out of my sight. In the jungle danger was always only a few steps away. There was one time when she was playing by the edge of the lake. I was trying to coax a few coconuts from a tree and I guess I wandered a bit farther away than usual. I was concentrating on dinner and looked up to see a full grown, male hippopotamus heading straight for my little girl.

Now, I don't know if you are familiar with hippos, behemoths so often depicted as clown-like and playful, but in reality they are nasty, with ugly dispositions, often attack without provocation and are, in my opinion, the most dangerous animal in the jungle. In addition, they are very territorial; once they claim a lake or a river, it is no longer safe, unless *they* allow you in.

Anyway, there I was, about two hundred yards away, and there she was about fifteen feet from this mean old hippo bearing down on her, mouth wide open, razor sharp tusks ready to scoop up my little Alena and drag her into the water. As I raced towards her not really sure what I could possibly do against such a beast, the hippo stopped, its mouth only inches from her head. I slowed down and slowly moved closer. She had her little hand on its wide nose and she was singing, a song I'd never heard before, in her native language. Whatever it was, the ugly brute was mesmerized. I slowly approached, but the hippo shook its head menacingly. She continued to sing and the hippo sat down next to her. From that day forward she was safe. No animal that lived in and around that lake dared cross that mighty hippopotamus. Of course, I still had to be careful.

Years passed and Alena grew tall and straight and beautiful. As she approached womanhood it didn't seem proper to have her going about naked; I fashioned a simple tunic for her from the skins of some animals. Of course, she objected to having to wear even that simple garment, but I had a plan for her and being naked was not part of it. I realized that as she became older she would need to be with people; truly, complete humans that could help her grow, love her, and share their lives. Living her life with a half-human freak of nature was not the path she was to take. I estimated she was about fourteen years old now and it was time to head north. I packed everything I thought we'd need and we started our journey, north and east, back towards Egypt, back to civilization.

6.

THE GOING WAS SLOW AT first. Alena was much bigger now and carrying her was a bit of a chore. She mostly walked with her hand on my side or shoulder, trusting me to find the way. But, despite the slow going, the journey was such an awakening for her. The new sounds and smells each brought excitement and wonder as her previously tiny world expanded. I was amazed as we walked along and she would tell me about a new bird and then point to its location on a tree branch above or perched on a craggy cliff.

"I'll bet that bird over there has bright feathers," she'd comment. "There's a snake to our right," she would add. And she was never wrong.

If we needed water, she would stop and listen, sniff the air and then point me in the proper direction. We were months making our way towards my old world and our path took us through Ethiopia, to the land called Sheba.

We made our way carefully, traveling mostly by night, something fairly easy for Alena, avoiding contact with the human population. Finally, we reached the outskirts of a large fortified city. We camped outside the gate while I contemplated the best way to approach the situation. As I saw it there were several options: Enter the city through the gate and hope that the people accepted us for what we were; avoid the city completely and continue on our journey north to Egypt or one of the other "civilized" nations, sneak into the city and explore it to see if it was an appropriate place for my dear Alena.

We saw people come and go, all with the same deep, dark complexion that Alena possessed; I also heard them speak Egyptian, which I spoke fluently and Alena understood and could also speak passably. After considering our options, I decided to take a chance on the city. I would enter the city as myself; my startling appearance would surely lessen the scrutiny of my young charge. I decided to cover her completely, to lessen the chance that there would be undo interest in her until the opportune time presented itself.

I managed to steal some women's clothes, cover Alena from head to toe and, with her safely tethered to my waist, I approached the gate. The city was surrounded by a great wall built from huge stones and solid wood, typical for those days, and the gate was formidable, solid wood and decorated with polished ivory and copper.

"Here goes nothing," I whispered to my young companion and I knocked on the gate with my solid walking stick. At first, no one answered, so I rapped on the gate again, this time with much more force. A small window opened and a white-haired man looked out, gave a short gasp, and then closed the window.

"I guess we're not welcome," I said loudly, but then I heard a low creaking noise and, to my great surprise, we were immediately ushered inside. We were greeted by "oohs" and "ahs" from a throng of gawking onlookers as we were beckoned to sit on two fine thrones, which were raised up by a dozen powerfully-built men who bore us towards the center of the city. As we passed by numerous ornately decorated buildings I saw why we had received such an auspicious welcome. There, in the center of the city, was a huge statue of me.

It wasn't exactly me; there was a bit more bull than I was made of and the face appeared far more fierce, but it was a Minotaur, cast in bronze, vanquishing a lion.

"There's a statue of a Minotaur killing a lion, but it must be my long lost cousin," I whispered to Alena. She smiled through her disguise, but didn't utter a word, being unable to truly understand all that was happening.

We were borne into the heart of the city where we came to a very fancy dwelling built of stone and tile with polished ivory and gold around its doors and windows. They carried us into a courtyard where we were instructed to stand before a much larger throne and await the arrival of the king.

We didn't have to wait very long as a young, muscular, and ornately-decorated man marched in with his head held high and took his seat on the throne. As soon as he sat down an older man placed a crown woven from gold and silver on his head. He looked at the older man as if to ask, "Do I really need to wear this stupid headgear?" but the elder merely bowed, very formally, as if answering by saying, "You have to look like a king if you're going to be king."

As for me, I wasn't sure if I was supposed to bow or kiss his hand (which would have been a bit of a trick for me), but he addressed me first, speaking Egyptian.

"Reports from Athens and Crete were that you were slain, mighty Minotaur. I can see that my spies are in error. Your absence has allowed Crete to be conquered by Athens. Are you here now to conquer Sheba?"

"I am here, Lord, to offer my humble services to you. Crete was no longer worthy and I abandoned that accursed island. I now return to your land and only ask for your acceptance," I answered, trying to sound humble.

"Who is it that accompanies you?"

"A young and very special maiden, Alena," I replied.

At the mention of her name, Alena did something remarkable and a bit rash, but, it turns out, she was far wiser and perceptive, in her blindness, than I ever could be. She whirled around and threw her disguise to the ground, leaving her standing naked before the great crowd and before the king.

She uttered a few noises, guttural sounds and then a louder roar like a lion. The people jumped back at this perfect mimicking of the king of beasts and, from the jungle outside there were roars that called out in response. She made some new sounds, birds and monkeys and, after a few moments, a flock of brightly covered birds descended and perched on her now outstretched arms, monkeys cascaded over the city wall and stood vigil around the courtyard. I chuckled at her remarkable display and I saw fear on the faces of the people around us, except on the king's face. He had a big smile and then started to laugh. He walked straight towards me and then past me, took off his crown, and placed it on Alena's head.

"Here is a true king," he exclaimed loudly to all the people around. "One who commands the world around us, one with true authority."

And he knelt at her feet, and, as he did this, all the people knelt. When he rose he waved his hand and one of his servants brought a majestic purple robe and draped it across her shoulders.

Finally, Alena spoke, "I am no ruler, no god, only a poor girl who should have perished long ago, except for the strength and kindness of my companion."

She moved forward and stood at my side.

I whispered, "They're all bowing down to you, maybe you should ask them to get up?"

She gestured for the king and his people to rise and she offered her arm to the young ruler who took it in his own and led her inside, leaving me standing alone, awkwardly, among all those people. After a few moments I followed the king and Alena, while the masses went about their daily business.

I found them inside chatting as if they were old friends. Alena spoke marginally good Egyptian and I could tell that the king spoke marginally good Greek. Between the two languages they didn't seem to be having any problem. I could tell that he had surmised that she was blind and she realized that he had a completely normal body, like hers, and was not a freakish chimera, like me. I suppose I felt a little hurt, although it was only natural for her to adapt so quickly. And, I could tell that the king really was lonely, that he'd been kept isolated. I approached them slowly and nonchalantly.

"I see that you two young people have hit it off quite well," I observed.

"You have the freedom of the palace, Minotaur, and my eternal gratitude," the king answered.

"Miny (that's what Alena called me), I'm so happy we came here. Thank you so much," she said and I sensed joy and elation in her voice, something she deserved. But I worried also, the worry a mother must feel when her only child is ready to leave the nest and make her way in the world.

I left the two of them together and set off to explore that fine palace.

7.

I T WAS AN OPULENT PLACE, even for those ancient times. There was room after room, with luxurious
mats piled high with furs in each. Water flowed from
ornate fountains and then out via troughs that eventually emptied into the river. Fresh fruits and vegetables were
stacked throughout and it was all strategically lit by amazing clean-burning lamps. I was accompanied by "servants"
(guards) as I made my way. I passed by one room where I
glimpsed a young woman a little older than Alena. She was
weeping loudly, while in the adjacent room the older man I'd
seen with the king spoke with one of the guards in hushed
tones. It didn't take an Einstein to figure out what was going
down. Undoubtedly, the weeping woman was in some way
promised to the king; Alena's untimely appearance seemed
to be interfering with these plans which somehow included
the older man, who I assumed was some sort of government
official. As we walked down the hall I casually asked one of
my escorts who the young woman was and if she needed help.

"That's Omaya. She was to be married to the king next
week. Her father is Moche, the man we saw talking with the
Captain of the Guard. He's the king's advisor."

It seemed to be a bit cliché, the whole scenario: king is
engaged to one maiden, maid's father hopes to profit by the
marriage, another girl comes along and the king is smitten
and the father now plots to get rid of his daughter's compe-
tition. We hadn't reached that part yet, but I was sure that

was to come next. I wish it had been that simple, but it was even a bit more complicated. The king, it seems, had been the first of triplets. He had a brother and a sister, either of whom stood to move up to the head position, if something happened to their brother.

The possibilities were endless and I imagined plotting more convoluted than the most intricate game of *Clue*. And, I didn't even know if the king had any intention of changing his wedding plans. In those days he could have as many wives as he wished. It was true that the first wife had some special priorities, but I was sure Alena didn't care about such things. I didn't even know if she had any feelings for the king. Maybe she was merely being polite, at least that's what I told myself. But as I walked by the main throne room again and saw the king and Alena still talking, now closer than ever, I knew. *The plot thickens*, I thought.

At this point there was only one fact that I could see that was clearly indisputable: the king and Alena were rapidly falling in love. The next logical fact to discern Omaya's true feelings. Was she in love with the king? I whistled for my two guards and went up the stairs and down the hall to her room where she was still crying softly. Luckily, neither her father nor the guards were around. I took this chance to make some discreet inquiries, starting with the soon-to-be jilted bride-to-be.

I went into her room and at the sight of me she stopped crying, stood straight up, and started to scream. At that moment, I let loose with a loud howl, which squelched her attempt to scream. Everyone, as expected, came running, and before Omaya could utter a word, I interjected.

"I was walking by this room and I saw this lovely maiden. I stopped to say hello and forgot that my unusual appearance would be startling, to say the least. But, when she jumped up so suddenly, why, it startled me and I let loose with that loud noise. I'm sorry."

I gave my voice a bit of a lilt and softened it to try to make it seem less threatening. I guess my explanation worked as everyone left us alone and I was able to talk.

"I saw you were sad, I'm sorry," I started. By this time her tears had dried and she was staring at me in a peculiar way.

"You look like a familiar beast. I've seen your likeness before. I know, in the courtyard," she remembered.

"Guilty," I said sheepishly.

"It was pretty obvious that I was upset; after all, I've done nothing but cry for the last two hours. My father is forcing me to marry that king. I don't love him. I want Sandoz, his twin brother."

At these words my face brightened, although my change in countenance was apparent only to me. I concluded that her ambitious father had arranged the marriage, but I also saw trouble ahead if the palace guard was loyal to her father. I quickly surmised that a little switcheroo would be in order. That would make almost everyone happy.

I suppose one would like to think that there was a great deal of intrigue and a complicated love triangle ensued, followed by a big comedy of errors and mishaps as one would expect of a Shakespearean comedy, until in the end, everyone ended up with who they wanted, the sinister father received his comeuppance and went off to live in a monastery, while all the love birds lived happily ever after.

That is not exactly what happened. My new role as matchmaker was short-lived and most definitely free of errors and mishap. All I did was go to each interested party, find out what he or she wanted, and then played messenger back and forth. The king clearly stated that he preferred Alena; Alena clearly expressed her desire to marry the king; Omaya and Sandoz declared their love for each; Atcha, the other royal sibling, said she didn't want to marry anyone, but would rather go travelling up north to Egypt or Canaan with me; even Moche said he didn't care who his daughter married as long as she was happy.

After a few hours of back and forth and a few final confirmatory meetings, everything was in readiness. There was a big double wedding; the brides looked ravishing, the grooms properly proud, and the overjoyed people of Sheba all in attendance. When it was over, only one task remained: to say goodbye to all of them, but particularly to Alena.

I waited a reasonable time, a couple of months, until she was settled and I was sure that she and the king were good for each other. Then, on a clear spring evening I asked her to walk with me in the palace garden.

"You are happy with the king," I stated, half asking, half a declaration of fact.

"Ecstatically, wonderfully happy. He's a good man and he is more than I ever dreamed of," she answered.

No surprise, I thought.

"I'm leaving. I have no purpose here," I told her.

"Miny, I always knew this day would come, only, I'd hoped it wouldn't be so soon," she sighed.

I reached up to my head and broke off the tip of my horn and poked a hole through the middle of it and placed it on a leather cord.

"This is part of me. Please wear it around your neck to remember me. Give it to you children and tell them the story. The story of an abandoned girl who was raised by a myth, lived and loved among the beasts of the jungle, and became Queen of Sheba."

She threw her arms around my neck and gave me a long hug and said, "I'll wear it always and I will never forget you. You're the best mother any girl could have had."

We parted at that moment. I grabbed my few belongings, called to Atcha, who was packed and ready to go, and we left, heading north towards Egypt, Canaan, Babylon, and other, as yet, undiscovered nations.

8.

TRAVELLING WAS QUICK AND EASY. All the people knew we were coming and homes were opened for us, particularly since I was with an actual princess. I decided to bypass Egypt and headed into Canaan. Coincidentally, the Israelites were getting ready to cross the Jordan River. I figured it had been at least forty years since I'd left them and I wondered what had taken them so long. I thought that Moses would be able to find his way better than that.

We watched them from the distance, camping on one side of the river, while on the other side was the walled city of Jericho. *That'll be a tough nut to crack*, went through my head. While I watched their camp I saw a strange light on the top of one of the mountains towering above. We left to investigate.

We climbed the far side of the mountain, so as not to be seen by the Israelites, but the going was slow. Atcha was not in the best of shape, after years of pampering in the palace and that northern side of the mountain was steep and rocky. I kept my eyes on the top, making sure that the unusual light up there remained. It reminded me of light I'd seen years ago, light at the top of a different mountain in a different desert.

Finally, we reached the summit and saw Moses sitting in the midst of the light, oblivious to our approach.

"Ahem... cough," I grunted trying to make our presence known. Moses opened his eyes, scowled, and then smiled. He had aged, his hair was thin and white, and his previously olive-toned skin was now a deeper brown baked into a wrinkled leathery covering.

"Y-you shouldn't be here," he said in a halting voice. "This is a place for death."

He wasn't startled by my appearance until I moved closer. His eyes had grown weak over the years, but when he finally could see me more clearly, he stopped and shouted, "You! ...you caused me so much grief, cost the lives of so many of my people! You deserve whatever God delivers."

"It's not right that you should be left here alone to die," I observed.

"Alone? D-do you think I am alone here? L-Look... look around, this is a holy place, God is in this place. Why did you come here; what brought you here? I'm sure it wasn't to stare at an old man on his deathbed. No, it was because you believed that God was here. I don't know if you are man or beast; perhaps there is no difference. But it is the man in you that looked up and saw a chance, a chance most men cower from. A chance most men have been offered over and over again, but reject over and over and over again. I believe there is some hope for you, Minotaur. As for you, young maiden," he said, moving closer to Atcha, studying her face, "you will become a great servant to Yahweh and one day will stand with Him in Paradise. Now, please, leave an old man in peace, but go with my blessing."

He laid his hands on both of us and then turned away and sat down as he had been seated before, closed his eyes, and was enveloped by the light, which now grew brighter and brighter. We turned and started to walk away, down the south side of the mountain. As we descended we saw the Israelites crossing the Jordan River, which had stopped flowing and was divided, just as the great Red Sea had been divided forty years before.

Atcha watched them crossing and I could see that she longed to join them, to be part of that new nation that was to rise across the Jordan. I smiled at her and nodded my head towards that throng of humanity and bid her farewell, then

I watched her run to the Israelites, confident in the words Moses had spoken, that she would be a great servant of their God. As for me, I felt out of place; I couldn't join the Israelites nor would it have been proper for me to stay on that mountain.

I left Moses and all humans and became a recluse, living alone as I had done years ago, once again it was my choice. Memories of the Labyrinth remained and I hated any spaces that confined. I chose to live in the hills away from all men, traveling throughout the Promised Land, watching the people grow, love, fight, triumph, and fail. I saw Joshua lead his people and defeat great Jericho.

Years later I heard of another great judge, a woman who had been a brave and resourceful warrior and now was leader of the tribes of Israel. Her name was Deborah, but when I ventured out of my seclusion to spy on that great nation, I saw that Deborah was none other than Atcha, who had left her nation to become a child of Israel and truly was a great servant of the Lord.

I watched and waited. I saw Gideon lead his people to victory. I saw David slay Goliath and become the great King. I cried for Uriah and marveled at Solomon. I saw the extravagant caravan carry the Queen of Sheba to Solomon and was gratified to see the tip of my horn adorning her neck. I thought of my dear Alena and how she had kept her promise, remembering me and how her descendants never forgot. I saw kings come and go. I saw the great nation split apart amid deceit and corruption and through it all I saw God's hand on his people, pushing them, nudging them towards righteousness, while the people only rebelled and rejected Him. Still, I stayed away, alone; how could I show up now? Who would remember the fierce Minotaur? I was a fading legend, soon to become myth. I was sure my time was ending, but the gods did not agree.

So, I survived. I stayed away from people, and the longer I stayed away the more my bovine half came to dominate. My hair grew longer to the point where it covered my body and I could pass for a true bull. I forgot all about men and hatred and lies and began to live among the cattle, grazing on tall grass, drinking from rivers, and sleeping under the stars. It was amazing how little attention the herders paid the animals. We roamed free and I truly felt free. But, I was never completely accepted by the bovine crowd. They saw me for what I was, a freakish human rather than a freakish bull.

The cows, or Elsies as I liked to call them, ignored me; the bulls threatened me, but I remained with them, one of the flock. I moved from herd to herd. For years I did my best to live as a bull, surrounded by so many others I tried to emulate, but my humanity always got in the way. I did manage to carve a special niche for myself among this cattle set: bovine midwife. It seems those cows that found themselves in the family way accepted me as someone who offered help. Not fully human and not fully bull, I think they considered me to be akin to a court eunuch, nonthreatening, someone sent to assist the Elsies through a sometimes difficult moment. And I delivered calves, hundreds over the years. Cows in labor seemed to show up out of nowhere, plop themselves down, and let me do all the work. I am proud to say that over the years I never lost one calf or mother.

I also have to say I sometimes wished I had been the father of one. I know it seems strange to outsiders, but there were some cows that I found very attractive, but most of them simply laughed their snorting laugh. After all, there was no way that I could compete with a true bull in the endowment department; that part of me was human.

I stayed a frustrated Minotaur for years and years and I almost forgot how to speak human languages. It was a freak occurrence and a near death experience that shook me up and sent me back to the world of men.

9.

THAT DAY STARTED LIKE SO many other days, I came out of hiding to join the other cows as they grazed outside the city. I'd been living with the cows for hundreds of years by now. The dogs came with the cows, herding, at least they thought they were doing a job, but the Elsies, the bulls and I just did as we pleased, but we shuffled our feet enough and made the proper mooing noises to make the dogs and the herders think they were in control.

Today was a bit different however, because besides the cows, there was a man, down on all fours acting like a cow. He was eating grass, mooing, behaving in every way like a bovine human. *Strange, very strange*, I thought. I went up to this man and whispered in his ear, "What's the deal, bud? What's with the cow routine?"

He ignored me and continued to eat grass. *He's crazy*, I thought, *how is a man to live on just grass?* But he did and it went on day after day after day, until the days became weeks and the weeks became months and then years. Some of the more fierce bulls didn't care for this newcomer and several times they tried to trample him or worse. It was a good thing I was there; I kept him out of harm's way, made sure he was protected from the elements; in short, I was his caretaker, nanny, and babysitter for years—a total of seven years.

During this time, important-looking men would occasionally come, look at the man, and then shake their heads. Often they tried to talk with him, but he just went right on eating grass, lying in the field, being a cow in all ways except his appearance and the fact that he was a man. I did try to talk to him; I told him that whatever was troubling him would pass and he would return to his home and family soon. I wasn't sure he understood me, but at times he would stop and stare, as if he was recalling happier days. Then the important-looking men would come and he would go right back to eating grass.

Then one day after years and years of this insanity, he stopped, abruptly spit out the grass, stood, and walked away. I was curious where he would go so I followed safely from a distance. As he walked he would stop every few minutes, turn, smile, and then continue on his way. I think he was checking on me. After going a few miles I realized that he was walking towards the palace. I sped up, thinking that he surely would be arrested and thrown into jail, or worse. I'd heard that the king, Neba something or other, was not one to be trifled with. As I got closer, some soldiers gathered around him. I stood up on my legs and started to run, trying to protect my bizarre friend. However, before I went twenty feet, *I was surrounded, tied up, and carried away. I'm in trouble!* swirled through my brain. *If they think I'm just a cow, I may just end up on a big platter roasted to medium rare.* These were my last thoughts before they whacked me over the head to keep me still as I was carried off to the slaughter house.

I awoke hanging upside down from the ceiling of a filthy, foul-smelling room with my bovine companions trussed up alongside. I couldn't see much hanging that way, but I could hear plenty and what I heard had me convinced that my days, no, *my minutes* were numbered.

About twenty feet away I heard a soft "swipe" and what sounded like running water accompanied by loud grunting protests from my doomed companions, protests which quickly faded to silence. The fetid smell of death filled the air as I anticipated the end that was rapidly approaching. Seeing no alternatives, I did something I'd never done before: I prayed; prayed to every god I'd ever heard of: Zeus, Poseidon, Hades, Yahweh, Baal, Isis, and every other real or false deity that had ever crossed into human imagination. At first I prayed silently, but the footsteps just moved closer and the executions continued; I started to pray out loud, softly, and then louder and louder. The footsteps stopped, probably wondering where the noise was coming from.

I saw the bloody feet standing next to me and there was no more mooing or braying in that slaughterhouse. I was next.

"If you spare my life I will grant you three wishes," I said with as much bravado as I could muster.

"Are... you... talking to me, cow," the executioner said in a very halting voice, as if this simple act of speech was beyond the capabilities of his limited mental capacity.

"Yes... yes, I am no simple cow; I'm the Minotaur and I have great power; set me free and you will be given everything you've ever dreamed of," I added, doing my best to keep him confused and to keep that razor sharp blade in its sheath.

"I don't know... uh... you're just a cow... uh... and... I need to have fresh meat for the feast. The Captain... uh... said the... uh... the king's returned."

"Of course the king's returned, I was the one that brought him home and he'll be plenty mad at you if you cut my throat. Where do you think he's been for the last seven years... Ethiopia? He's been with me; I've been looking out for him. You better let me go if you know what's good for you."

"But you're just a dumb cow."

"Could a dumb cow talk to you like this?"

"I... it's just a ... a trick... yup, a dumb trick."

At this moment the door to the slaughter house flew open and half a dozen burly, very mean-looking guards came in, walked directly towards me and cut me down. They didn't say a word, but pushed me ahead of them. I walked out upright. As I was led out, I stuck out my tongue at that simpleton of an assassin (childish, I know).

"It's a good thing these guys came along when they did, or else you'd find yourself strung upside down with your throat sliced open," I said loudly as I was ushered out.

The guards led me to a side door entrance to the palace where I waited in a small room, for the king I presumed. An elderly man brandishing scissors, a razor, some knives, and a bunch of bags entered and approached.

"I'm the king's barber, Simon Joseph. He has sent me to clean you up before he grants you an audience," he remarked.

Grant me an audience, after all I did for him? Some gratitude. I started to protest, but refrained. He is the king and has to maintain proper appearances, I figured. A shave and haircut would do me good, especially since it had been years.

I sat in the chair and Simon went to work, and boy, did he work! Scissors, razors, knives, soap, and various creams went this way and that, hair started to pile up on the floor, and in no time at all he was finished. He brought me a mirror where I could, for the first time in eons, look at myself. I almost looked human. My horns were neatly polished to a bright shine, my face looked nearly human, hair that had grown long enough to cover my human half was trimmed and groomed and laced with blue ribbons and scented with a fine, manly perfume. While I was admiring myself a voice called to me.

"You are far more human than cow," the voice said.

I turned around to see the same man I'd tended and protected for the last seven years, standing straight and tall, dressed in fine silk and adorned with golden armor. I tried to remember my protocol and bowed deeply, but he ran to me and embraced me.

"I owe you my life. I would have perished many times over if not for your watchful eye. You are the Minotaur, I presume? The legends surrounding your name are in error, I believe."

We sat together and I told him my story. I also learned that he was King Nebuchadnezzar; at that time the most powerful ruler in the world. His empire spanned most of civilization and here I sat, his nursemaid for the last seven years; *a bit of irony*, I thought.

"It was the God of the Hebrews that humbled me, but also restored me. This God is now my God," he told me.

"I'm glad you have a God to believe in. If there is a God out there, He abandoned me long ago," I observed. "Living among humans or cows; there isn't any real difference. Humans use you and then toss you away like yesterday's trash; the cows threaten and leave you outcast. The truth is that I don't think there's any place for me or those like me. Half breeds, be they human or beast, will always be outsiders. I'm glad this God has restored you, but He has done nothing for me. I think I've been most happy when I've been left alone, in solitude."

"Is that what you wish, Minotaur, solitude?"

"I... I just don't know," I answered truthfully. "So many of the people I've met have been nothing but cruel. A few have been kind, but I know that if I stay here, with you, someday, someone will hurt me. That's why I'm going away."

"I see your mind is made up. I will not stand in your way. Will you leave soon?"

"Tomorrow, I think, perhaps go north or maybe east to the Orient."

"I wish you well, Minotaur. I will see that you have safe passage as long as you are within my kingdom. Goodbye and thank you."

He hugged me and slowly walked away, turning briefly to smile and wave. For my money, he was a fine man.

10.

I LEFT BABYLON AND HUMANITY and moved back to what had been Canaan, living as a hermit in what has politely been called the wilderness. Sand and scorpions and hot wind became my companions as I avoided people. People had caused me so much pain and sadness, although I wasn't sure why I felt this way. I assumed it was because I was different and I suppose I struck fear in some of them, but just as many had shown me love and kindness. I was more confused than anything. I didn't fit in with humanity or bovinity. If I was destined to live a life of solitude, I preferred it be one of my choosing. By this time it was clear that I had been blessed with long life, perhaps immortality. I'd now been alive for several hundred years and was still in peak physical condition; mentally and psychologically, however, I was a mess. It appeared that long life carried a price, in my case, recurring episodes of deep depression.

I lived in what would be southern Israel today, the southern end of Canaan in the hills and in the desert. I didn't see another human or cow for hundreds of years. Occasionally, I heard a caravan coming and I would stay hidden until it was safely past. I found that my dietary needs were minimal, desert flowers, various insects, snakes and such made for passable nutrition. I vaguely remember passing time drawing on the sides of large rocks, images of myself, horses, cows, my dear Alena, and anything else that popped into my head. Over the years I'd learned to play the lyre and I spent time gently, quietly teasing its strings, music that soothed and healed. The hot days and cold nights were only a minor annoyance; my long hair provided pretty good insulation.

But, like all good and not-so-good things, such a life could not last. After hundreds of years, it ended. I saw a man, a solitary figure wandering through the wilderness lost and, I figured, destined to die. *Let him find his own way,* I thought, but still I watched him. I followed the man for days and days, staying hidden. And, although that man was alone, I always had the sense that there was someone nearby, someone besides me, keeping watch and keeping him safe. I'm not sure what it was, perhaps it was the stars which seemed to shine brighter at night, or the moon which shined on his head in the early morning when he kneeled and prayed to his unseen God, or the clouds which offered shade from the scorching days for no reason.

Something told me that this lone man was to be the central figure in an elaborate and important morality play that was to be performed away from any audience, save me and the snakes and scorpions. Days passed and he still wandered, going nowhere, but always with a sense of purpose. I don't think I ever saw him sleep or eat; he just walked and walked.

After forty days I was about to give up my pursuit; walking and praying, praying and walking, did not make for compelling theater. But after so many days the play unfolded. The man was no longer solitary; another actor appeared. This new character was thin and pale, dressed in fine robes, which sharply contrasted with the now ragged garment the man wore. This new character sat on a large rock, while the solitary man had an angry look on his face.

From my distant vantage point I couldn't hear the conversation, but the newcomer stood tall as if he held some authority and held up some rocks, pointing to them while speaking.

The other man looked angry, shook his head and gestured, finally pointing to the sky. At that moment, the finely clad interloper touched the other's shoulder and they disappeared.

I was startled by this sudden, unexpected event and I stood up and ran to that place, half expecting to find some wondrous sign. What I did find was two freshly baked loaves of bread, untouched and very tempting. I gathered them up, not sure if I should keep them for the man if he should return, or eat them myself.

I thought about these events for weeks, kept those loaves of bread until they were dried out and hard, finally burying them in the desert sand. Funny thing happened: A huge tree sprang up in the very same spot where I buried that bread, almost overnight, with broad spreading branches and bright green leaves. I'd say that tree was a bit of an anomaly, bright green in the midst of all the browns and grays that make up the desert. That place became a sort of tourist attraction, as the following spring that remarkable tree bore sweet red fruit of a type never seen before or since.

Anyway, outside of that tree, all traces of those men vanished and I went back to my old ways. It was about three years later that I saw that same, solitary man again, still solitary, in a sense, even though he was surrounded by people.

I don't know why I left the safety and seclusion of the wilderness. I had a sense that something was happening that I should at least witness. I travelled north to the outskirts of the city called Jerusalem. That's where I saw the same man, only now he had been beaten, the huge crowd was yelling at him, save for a few who wept. The man trudged along, bloody, dirty, almost dead, but I saw his eyes and, well, those eyes told the whole story. His body may have been broken, but he was not defeated. There was a sense of purpose in those eyes, a look of determination. And, then I looked at the throng of people taunting him and they all looked the same to me; they all looked like the pale character that had confronted this man in the wilderness. What happened next saddened me. The mass of people reached the top of a hill where that man and two others were laid on top of wooden crosses and nailed to them as if they were some sort of wall adornment. I'd heard of this practice, but it was the first and only time I ever saw it performed and, well I couldn't help myself. I turned to the side and threw up.

I saw them stand the wooden crosses upright. Above the man's cross I saw some words, but I was too far away to read what was written. At that moment, I heard shouting and then I was struck by a stone and then more stones. I looked up and saw a mob of boys and young men coming towards me. Their eyes were full of hatred and I sensed that I was in real danger. I got up and ran, but they pursued me, each brandishing sizeable stones. They were screaming now and they split into two groups.

I'm in trouble! ran through my head, but as I darted around a large boulder I saw a cave and I ducked inside. *Maybe I'll be safe in here*, I thought as I moved to the back, as far from the entrance as possible. Still, light poured in from outside and I was sure they would find me. At that moment the light became darkness. Not just the darkness of a large cloud blocking the sun, no, this was middle-of-the-night darkness. And I heard rumbling as if there was an earthquake, but the ground didn't shake. Whatever was happening saved me, because the angry mob of youthful hatred never returned.

A few hours later there was a noise in the front of the cave. Some men came and gently laid a package on the cave floor before quickly exiting. Then I heard another noise, only this was a scraping sound and it became pitch black inside. A large stone had been rolled in front of the cave's entrance. I was trapped.

Silence enveloped the room. I held my hand up in front of my face, but I couldn't see even the tiniest gleam of light. I felt my way towards the front, to the spot where the entrance had been, and I pushed with all my strength; I may as well have been trying to push the moon out of orbit. I felt the package that the men had deposited on the cold, solid rock floor. There was soft cloth around what I soon realized was a corpse. It was cold, stiff, and lifeless. *This is quite a predicament, worse than the Labyrinth.* I sat down next to my lifeless companion and started to think.

I sat for a long time, hours, days, there was no way to know. Every once in a while I stood up, felt the hard, cold walls of my prison, pushed against the large stone and then sat down. *This is going to be the end.*

After I don't know how long, something happened, a miracle really, at least for me. After having wasted my strength for about the hundredth time trying to move the stone that blocked my escape, a light appeared. It started at the top of my tomb and filled the whole cave. I moved to the back of the cave again as bright light, brighter than the sun, illuminated that lifeless body and, after a while, a lone figure appeared, neither man nor woman, an angel I presumed. This angel reached out his hand, and the soft shroud fell away and the man arose, clothed in bright white light. He looked right at me and smiled. He walked towards me. I wasn't sure what I should do, but I assumed He was some sort of god, so I knelt down. Silently, He touched my head and I felt a warmth come over me. After this act, the inside of the cave became so bright I couldn't open my eyes. I heard Him walk to the entrance as the light started to fade. I opened my eyes and saw Him push against that great stone with one hand; He brushed it aside as if it was a feather and He walked away. The light had completely vanished.

I made my way to the front of the cave and saw that the entrance was wide open. I waited about ten minutes and then I exited. There were two Roman guards outside, both stiff, as if they were frozen. The man was gone and I decided it was time for me to be gone, too.

I knew there'd be trouble if I was discovered. The days when a freak like me could live in polite society seemed to have passed.

I'll go away, head North, away from civilization, I decided. It was early morning and I saw two women coming towards that tomb. I quickly made my escape, but as I started to leave I stopped and went back to the cave. I looked inside, saw the empty shroud. I looked at the great stone that the man had pushed away as if it were a pebble and I felt the warmth that started with the touch of his hand, but now filled my soul. I silently offered a prayer of thanksgiving and then I left.

11.

I WASN'T SURE WHERE TO go, but I knew I wanted to leave that land. I thought about returning to Crete, visit my old home and see if the Labyrinth was still there. I hitched a ride on a Roman galley working as a taskmaster over the condemned slaves. The Roman soldiers weren't very picky about who they employed when it came to lording over their slaves. Most of the slaves seemed oblivious to my unusual appearance, most likely overwhelmed by their own misery.

As luck would have it, a storm blew us well past Crete and the ship's captain decided to sail for Rome instead. After a few weeks we docked near that great city and I said my goodbyes. I had made some friends on board and they directed me to the Coliseum. They said I'd find a man who could use a body with my particular talents and attributes. I sought out Claudius Tobius, who—as it turned out—managed a stable of gladiators. He took one look at me and nearly fell over, effusively saying that he surely could use a man with my skills. That's not exactly what he said; I believe it was more along the lines of, "A beast like you will scare the other gladiators right out of their tunics."

Up until this time I really hadn't been much of a fighter and I tried to politely decline, but he wouldn't take no for an answer. He gave me a room, conveniently locked from the outside "to prevent unwanted visitors," he said. He only fed me a little bit at a time, really no concern; I was used to going long periods of time eating little or nothing. He brought a sword, shield, and spear to my room and left them, telling me to practice, practice, practice. He even sent a man, Augustus was his name, to teach me the finer points of combat. I still wasn't much of a fighter, but I tried my best. Augustus had been a soldier until he was hurt in a battle against the barbarians up North. One of his hands had been cut off, so his usefulness as a soldier ended and he was given the job of preparing gladiators for combat in the arena. I don't think I was a very good pupil.

Still, we got along famously. He told me stories of his exploits in battle and I told him my story; I also taught him to read and gave him a beginner's course in philosophy, along with some history—at least the history according to the Minotaur, which may have been less than accurate. All in all, however, we helped each other considerably.

The most important thing he taught me was the art of surprise; doing the unexpected to give yourself an edge. For instance, he told me that the biggest advantage I would have in the arena was my unusual appearance and the fear that could be generated. We fashioned a special helmet, one that covered not only my head, but also my shoulders, but also was easy to remove. In the heat of battle I could rip this head covering away, causing my opponent to pause as he gazed on my unusual, but altogether regal countenance, and thus afford me the opportunity to vanquish my surprised foe. Vanquishing my foe, that was another sticky point. As I'm sure you realize by now, I am not, and never have been, a killer. Entering the arena, a kill-or-be-killed situation presented a bit of a moral dilemma for me. Through all this training I wasn't sure how I would handle it. I thought about hanging a sign around my neck: "Conscientious Objector," but I was afraid my opponent would lack the proper sense of humor and I'd end up with a spear in my left ear. After some very serious thought I decided that my best bet was to be the best; to be so thoroughly superior to my adversaries that they would be left to my mercy.

Luckily, I had a really fine teacher. Augustus, despite his disability, knew all the finer points of combat. He taught me how to stay balanced, how to develop my "sixth sense"—the ability to be aware of everything that was happening at all times and have some awareness of an enemy's presence whether I was reading a book, bathing, or asleep. He used to try to sneak up on me at the most inconvenient moments and I had to be ready to defend myself. Sort of reminds me of the *Pink Panther* movies. Augustus would cut a notch in my horn if he successfully took me by surprise. I have to say that I only had a couple of notches. Well, maybe four.

I was much better at direct combat. Swordplay was child's play, the shield had its appeal and I had no fear of the spear. (Sorry about the bad poetry, sometimes I can't resist). After a few weeks of training the word came that I was to appear in the arena the next day, ready or not.

"You're as ready as any man or beast could be," Augustus declared. "With the element of surprise, I don't think you'll have any problem. It's your first time, so I expect you'll get something easy, a couple of dwarfs or one of the older Gladiators that they're trying to bump off, you know, thinning the ranks."

"Well, I'm ready, thanks to my excellent coach," I replied. I didn't tell him that I had no intention of killing anyone. There was no need and it all seemed so barbaric.

That night, as I tossed and turned, I thought about all that I'd been through, how many lifetimes I'd lived, and I contemplated a future—my future—fighting other unfortunates until I was killed. I thought about the man in the cave, still wondering why he had left me with such profound and unsettled feelings. To this day I don't understand it. As the night dragged on and the dawn started to peek through my window I finally sat up in my bed and I went to the window and looked out at the rising sun. *Is this to be my last sunrise?* I thought. I was never one for praying, but at that moment I slumped to the floor and stared at the dusty stone.

"God, if you are there, tell me what's to become of me. Is this my last day? Will I be forced to choose: kill or be killed? Why did you make me like this? Why have you kept me here for so long? At least, please God, grant me peace."

I looked up at the sun, now brighter and blinding, but it was an empty vessel. There was no peace and I was sure it would be the end no matter what happened. I heard the door opening and stood up, dusting my knees as Augustus walked in.

"A common sight among soldiers preparing for battle and Gladiators about to enter the arena. You'll be fine. It's your first time; they'll go easy on you. It'll be condemned slaves or a scared wild beast. Believe me; you won't be facing Flavius Maximus, that's for sure."

"Flavius Maximus?"

"Flavius Maximus, the current champion, the Emperor's favorite. He's a big, dark-skinned man, very adept with the sword and spear. He's been in the arena for over two years and has barely suffered a scratch. I don't think they'll waste you on him."

A guard came with my breakfast and we talked a great deal about nothing for a while until it was time to leave. I stared at my room as I walked away. *I don't think I'll miss it one bit. It's just an old dusty room. I'm sure I'll go to a better place.* As this thought ran through my head I glanced up at the sun, then I closed my eyes as Augustus and the guard dressed me in my "gladiator" costume.

"I haven't been able to learn who your opponent will be, which is just as well, I don't want you to be disappointed when you end up fighting a couple of midgets. Maybe they'll send a couple of condemned criminals your way, always an easy day's work..."

Augustus kept up a nonstop stream of inane chatter as we started up the stairs to the arena and they strapped on my last armored plate and special helmet. A voice grew louder as we neared the top.

"...and the main event, a newcomer, Quintus, will battle our never defeated champion Flavius Maximus."

A loud roar almost knocked me over as I entered the arena as the door was closed and locked behind me. I glanced behind and saw Augustus shaking his head, white as the finest alabaster. *Probably thinking that all his hard work was going to be wasted in one short duel; he's probably right.*

I shook these thoughts out of my head as I looked up to see a huge black man. A gold ring pierced each of his ears while the rest of his face was hidden by a helmet and mask. He must have been six and a half feet tall, solid muscle, and he wielded a long, heavy, shiny sword. There was a knife in his belt, a spear on his back, and a shield with—ironically—the head of a bull engraved upon it. It was a very hot day and the sun was high in the sky. The heat made my opponent's skin glisten with sweat while it made me uncomfortable inside my huge helmet.

Flavius eyed me briefly as I stood about thirty feet away trying to convince my terrified, frozen feet to run back to the now-locked escape door. I fumbled for my sword, but dropped it as I pulled it from its sheath. As I groped in the dirt to retrieve my wayward blade I heard a whoosh in my right ear as a spear big enough to skewer the shark from *Jaws* sailed past and lodged in the dirt to my right. I managed to pick up my sword just in time as Flavius charged towards me brandishing his powerful weapon. I held up my sword and my shield, cringing as a powerful blow crashed down, shattering my wooden shield into a thousand future toothpicks.

That's it, I'm done for, I thought as I looked up and saw the razor sharp edge raised high, about to deliver the *coup de grace*.

Do something, anything! I lashed out with my foot and delivered a sharp kick to his shin. He paused for a split second and then he brought his weapon down. I managed to roll to the side as the blade caught the edge of my armor and there was a loud clang. I jumped to my feet and grabbed him around his narrow waist as he pushed his shield into my face.

"Can't we talk this over?" I asked. "Let's be reasonable. I mean, we haven't even been properly introduced."

He tried to shake me loose and then he spoke.

"Duh," was all he said.

I managed to look through his mask into his eyes and it was at that point I realized I was in big trouble. Here was a man in size only. Behind those eyes was utter blankness. He probably only knew one thing, which was kill or be killed. As I maintained my grasp around his waist I saw scars, ugly healed scars going every which way on his arms, chest, legs, feet, and back. The evidence of years of abuse that had turned him into more beast than human. Then I looked at his shield. The creature engraved upon it was no mere bull, but me—the fierce Minotaur.

I pushed Flavius away with all my might and then stood upright. Now nearly as tall as my opponent, I ripped off my helmet. Flavius, who had started to charge towards me stopped as I stood there, my arms outstretched, all my weapons scattered in the dirt of the arena floor. I did my godlike best to be intimidating and I must have succeeded. The roaring of the crowd stopped as a collective gasp and then silence swept through the stands. A very confused Flavius suddenly stopped and stared, then he tore off his helmet, revealing his face; a face twisted by years of abuse. One cheek bone was completely sunken, pulling his right eye down and contorting his mouth into a permanent sneer, while his nose was flattened, almost nonexistent. His eyes were deeply bloodshot and there was a stream of spit that ran from the corner of his mouth. When he saw me he fell to his knees with his distorted face buried in the loose soil. Straight ahead of me was the Emperor who seemed to tremble slightly as I stared boldly, directly into his supposedly divine eyes.

I slowly walked towards Flavius, who was now weeping like a newborn babe, and I gently lifted his face out of the ground, wiped the dirt and tears away, and took his hand. He stood beside me as we approached the royal box. The Emperor, his eyes squinting and his shaking thumb held sideways, stood up and, with a quick jerk, turned his thumb straight down, signaling for the kill. Flavius, who was still carrying his magnificent sword, turned and looked at me, then looked at his shield and finally at the Emperor. He looked straight into my eyes as he buried his sword deep into the blood red sand that covered the arena floor. With this act of defiance a dozen guards raced from unseen corners, shackled both of us and led us away to await a punishment that I suspected would be far worse than being forced to fight as gladiators.

12.

W E SPENT THAT NIGHT TOGETHER, chained to the wall in my new companion's "room," which was truly more of a prison than even my sparse room. Flavius said nothing as the door was slammed shut and bolted. His contorted face betrayed no feeling as I tried to discern his state of mind.

"It looks like we're in big trouble now," I said, stating the obvious. "We'll end up feeding the lions or at the end of an oar for sure."

"Uh... uh," was all the reply I received.

"Is that all you have to say?" I asked, annoyed.

My reply must have struck a nerve because he reached out with his chained arm and grabbed my horn, pulling my head around until I was staring into his face. He opened his mouth as far as he could, which wasn't very far, and stuck out the scarred remnant of what had been his tongue.

Inside and out, I thought. I reached out as best as I could and patted his shoulder.

"OK, I guess I'll do all the talking," I said in a soft voice. "Although I suspect we won't have to worry about talking or thinking for very long. The Emperor won't stand for such outright defiance from his most trusted generals, let alone a couple of misfit gladiators. He'll surely want our heads on a platter."

At that moment there was some noise from outside, jangling of keys, and then a slow creaking as the heavy door opened.

"A fine fighter you turned out to be," a familiar voice exclaimed. Augustus stood in front of me, eyeing us both up and down. "And you, Flavius, the great champion, startled by your opponent's unusual appearance."

"Not startled, Augustus, more confused," I interrupted. "Look around this cell and you'll understand."

Augustus did look around, silently. There was almost nothing in Flavius's "room." A pile of old straw, a thin blanket, an old wooden bucket, a cold stone floor, and little else except, standing proudly in the corner, a statue of me. I was a god again, at least in the eyes of this lost champion. That explained the image on his shield and his reluctance to make me into a Minotaur Kabob in the arena.

Just delayed the inevitable, was all that I could think at that moment.

Augustus looked me sternly in the eye before speaking. "I've intervened with the Emperor on your behalf, both of you. The Divine One owed me a favor. Instead of sending you off to the galleys, he will allow you to accompany me to the north, to join our illustrious Roman fighting men in their battles to conquer the savage people that stand ready to invade our world. I managed to persuade His Grace that sending two such accomplished fighting men to the galleys would be a supreme waste of valuable resources. Although in your case," he stared at me, "my words were a bit of an exaggeration. So, the three of us are off to battle the barbarians."

"You're going back into battle?" I asked incredulously.

"I'm ten times the fighter you'll ever be, even with only one good arm. Besides, the Emperor doesn't trust you. Neither do I, if you must know the truth. And, I don't want to spend my days training reluctant gladiators in the fine arts of combat only to see them sent to their doom. Maybe I'm just not very good at it. Anyway, I convinced our noble leader that I should escort you to the battlefields in the north. We leave at daybreak."

With these words the guards unshackled us and brought some fresh food and water. The two of us lay down on that hard floor and quickly passed into deep sleep. I'm not sure why I felt it, but I had the feeling that I would be safe under the watchful eye of my giant, silent, newly found companion.

The following morning we started out on our journey north, aiming to rendezvous with the Roman army that was in a never-ending battle with various Germanic tribes. I have to say that we looked pretty spiffy in our brand new, custom made Roman uniforms. Augustus and Flavius sported shiny metal helmets which reflected blinding light in the bright mid-morning sun as we started out, red plumage flapped back and forth with the morning breeze. We carried only the barest essentials: weapons, two days provisions, supplies for the horses, and a tent. With Augustus in the lead and with minimal fanfare, we started on what was to be a mostly uneventful trip into the barbarous lands up north.

The journey did have one highlight, what I call the great wild boar hunt. We were somewhere in southern Gaul; I guess we'd been on the road three or four days. We'd already used up our provisions, and although we'd killed a few rabbits and found some truly delightful mushrooms, my companions wanted something a bit more substantial. We saw the beast foraging through an open field. Augustus immediately signaled Flavius and the two split up and disappeared, leaving me more than a bit confused.

Well, there was a rustling of bushes and then some shouting. A few moments later, charging from the bushes was one very angry wild boar, bearing right down on me. I swear that beast was straight out of Hell. His eyes gave off a red glow and he had huge, sharp tusks. I'm positive there was smoke and fire shooting out of his nostrils. The monster was apparently in a most foul mood. I guess the prospect of ending up on a spit with an apple stuffed in your mouth, roasting away can dampen even the brightest spirit. So, there I was, sitting on my horse, no fancy helmet or anything, and this demon from Hell coming straight for me.

What to do? Well, what would anyone do? I took off in the opposite direction. As I raced away I heard shouting and whooping as Augustus and Flavius took up the chase.

"Use your spear, you big oaf, skewer that sucker," Augustus yelled as he picked up his spear.

"Easy for you to say, he's not trying to turn *you* into shish kebob," I yelled back. As I finished this retort, Flavius burst out of some thick underbrush and turned directly into the wild boar's path. He let fly with his big heavy spear and stopped that pig right in its tracks as the lance found its mark in its neck. When that beast fell to the ground I heard laughter coming from behind me.

"I fine fighter you are. Didn't I teach you anything?"

I turned to Augustus and answered, "I am as I was made. You can dress me up, but in the end, I'll always be the quiet intellectual."

"Well, tell that to the barbarians."

My two companions feasted on roast pork that night. I was content to stick with my mushrooms.

The remainder of the trip north was quiet: no marauders, no wild animals, no barbarians, just the occasional rain shower and some very annoying insects. We arrived at the Roman outpost as ready as we could be. Augustus and Flavius didn't get a taste of combat right away. Instead, Augustus had to take over command of the garrison.

13.

THE ROMAN TROOPS SERVING AT that distant outpost were not what I would call "elite." I soon discovered that this "army" was composed of outcasts, criminals, and freaks. A Roman officer with one hand, a man with the head of a bull, and a big, dark, speechless Ethiopian fit right in. Augustus, as ranking officer, took over as commander. The previous leader, Octavius, seemed very happy to relinquish the purple robe that identified him as the man in charge. Made perfect sense to me; who wants to be a target?

Augustus went right to work, doing his best to whip this crew into a cohesive disciplined fighting unit. In the beginning, the best he could do was to keep the "soldiers" from fighting with each other. He turned to Octavius for help, but found the former commander drunk far more often than sober. Luckily our German adversary was in the process of regrouping. Apparently, we had just missed a vicious battle and, although they were a motley, ill-disciplined band, the Roman soldiers were also fierce and fearless. The Germans were off licking their wounds, but, as I was told over and over, the battle would never end until either we were all dead or vice versa. Something about the whole process didn't sit right with me. We were defending Rome, but why should these outcasts care one bit about the Roman Empire? I assumed they were all given a choice: fight for Rome or die. I also assumed that the only end point was death. As long as they fought well and served Rome's purpose they survived, but one slip up and it was over. I also learned that the only chance for freedom was a note of clemency from the Emperor, something that had never been issued for a member of this garrison. Hopeless men, fighting for a nation they could only hate, with their only prospect the continuous hell of war or death; no wonder morale and discipline were so poor.

The first few weeks were nothing but boring. Augustus did his best to instill some sense of discipline, the soldier in him convinced that well-drilled, disciplined soldiers were the only truly effective and happy soldiers. At first the men tried, but those soldiers' limited prospects did little to motivate them. Augustus finally found the proper inspiration, however. He decided that any spoils earned from the fight would be divided amongst the men. This included any and all valuables, food and wine, clothing and prisoners, particularly women. I found the whole sordid business abhorrent, but then I had never had quite the same desires or drives as normal men and I had suffered more than my share of rejection from people and cows. However, this new stimulus definitely served its purpose with the troops. The men learned to follow commands, how to march in formation, and to help each other in hand-to-hand combat. They truly became a well-oiled fighting machine.

One "soldier" was less than thrilled with Augustus and his methods of training and inspiration. Mobus was the Emperor's envoy, his spy, more or less; he reported directly to the Emperor. *His* only motivation was to please the Emperor and the prospect of distributing what rightfully would be the Emperor's (and his) spoils did not sit well with little Mobus. I say little because Mobus was very short, only 4 foot 8 inches tall with a high squeaky voice, which was annoying to say the least. The men barely tolerated him. For the most part they did their best to avoid any contact with him. They assumed that any "interference" with the Emperor's little spy would be met with swift and severe punishment. They decided, and Augustus seemed to concur, that it was best to ignore the troublesome gnat, shoe him away if he became annoying, but otherwise tolerate his presence.

Back to the war, which I really hadn't yet experienced. The barbaric German tribes were our enemies, supposedly huge in stature, fierce in nature, and totally without mercy or redeeming values. The Roman Senate saw them as blight upon the world, uncivilized and unredeemable. Our task was to completely and utterly annihilate these presumably beastly persons. There was only one problem at that moment. We didn't have the foggiest notion where they were. Outside of all their unredeemable qualities, they did possess a great talent for staying hidden. I suspected, as did the rest of the troops, that they were always about, spying on us, trying to annoy us. Guards at night heard rustling when there wasn't any wind, birds and animals calling for no reason, trees fell blocking our way seemingly out of spite. They were around, that much was for sure. And Augustus decided that waiting for *them* to make the first move was a waste of valuable time. He devised a plan to bring them out into the open and force a fight, one he was sure we would win. Unfortunately, I was the bait. That's the trouble with being the Minotaur. Every one treats you as if you're half bull. Anyway, he planned for the battle with the next full moon, two days away.

I spent those two days with Flavius. Despite his speaking difficulties, I understood him as clearly as if he were Winston Churchill. We talked about Africa and Ethiopia. Here are the highlights of his life:

"I was the best runner in my tribe. I could run forever, never felt tired. Always ran barefoot, but pebbles and thorns never seemed to bother my feet. I guess I had a lot of sole.

"I was supposed to marry an Ethiopian princess; instead, I ended up a Roman slave.

"You and I have a lot in common, very different from those around us, outcasts and always misunderstood. You are far too sensitive; it will be the end of you someday.

"I'm sure I'm destined to die in this forsaken wasteland, all I want is to die doing something worthy."

He was a good friend to me, a kind soul and truly was a gentle giant. But, he was wrong about dying.

Two days passed by and it was time to engage our enemy. Under the light of the full moon the plan was set into motion and I was worried.

The plan was not elaborate and it was not particularly deceptive. I was to play the role of a wayward bull and lure the enemy into the open while our troops waited in ambush. I was made up to look cow-like, to appear vulnerable, and put into a clearing where I made cow noises.

"Moo... moo," I crooned. "Moooo... moo... mooooo." I almost broke into song.

I went on like this for an endless time. It seemed like hours, although I suppose it was only about fifteen minutes. I was ready to give up when the bushes began to rustle. *This plan is really going to work? Unbelievable!* I was thinking when there was a rush from the bushes to my right. About thirty Germans rapidly descended upon me, threw a rope around my neck, and started to drag me away. Per the plan I put up a bit of a fight and started to moo even louder.

"MOO... MOOOOO... MOO... hey you guys, MOO!" I let slip. *Uh oh.*

The Germans stopped and stared at my words and started to high tail it out of there when my guys charged from the bushes whooping and hollering. The fighting started, while I tried to slink out of harm's way. As I began to make my escape a second wave of barbarians descended upon the clearing and I realized that it was an ambush indeed, only my guys were the ambushees. There was a diminutive figure, covered from head to toe in shiny armor, at the front of this second wave, calmly issuing orders. I started to warn my comrades when I felt a sharp blow on the top of my head and everything went black.

I don't know how long I was out, but when I finally came to I was in the German encampment, wrapped in heavy rope inside a tent made of animal skins. There was a torch burning, illuminating my prison with smoky light. There was a guard standing by the entrance, a tall blonde man wearing a metal breast plate, armed with a spear and sword. There was a second, almost identical guard outside the doorway. I gave the expected struggle to free myself from the heavy bonds, gave up after five minutes, and then relaxed. I was sure there would be someone coming soon to interrogate me. Before long, their captain appeared, still covered from head to toe in armor. I was able to see that he had dark, almost black hair, and was far shorter than the guards. *Certainly not physically imposing, must be a brilliant tactician,* I thought. He started to question me, but his voice was muffled by his helmet.

"I can't understand you very well," I stated as politely as I could.

The great leader paused for a moment and then pulled off "his" helmet. Long black hair fell to "his" shoulders, and I saw that he was a she, with a slight build, a dark complexion, and beautiful dark eyes. Definitely not Germanic, but more Roman, really. It wasn't long before I learned just how Roman she was.

"The Romans really are rounding up the dregs of society," she stated in perfect Latin as she walked around me. "What kind of freak are you? Are you a man... or a monster?"

I thought about my options at this point. Should I play the injured stoic and remain silent, or, perhaps, the defiant warrior, which was definitely not my style. I just decided to be myself and see what transpired.

"I am the Minotaur, young lady, perhaps you've heard of me, famed for being the vicious inhabitant of the dread Labyrinth on the isle of Crete."

As I finished, a tall blond guard rapped me across the head with the side of his sword.

"Hey," I screamed, "that hurt!"

"You will address me as 'General,' or 'sir,' or even 'boss,' but not 'young lady.' Do you understand, Minotaur?" she asked sternly. Still, I detected a smirk in her voice.

"Yes, sir, boss. You're not a young lady. I understand, General."

My sarcasm brought me another rap on the head.

"Well, Minotaur, you are our prisoner. I hope you like the accommodations. If you try to escape, I've left strict orders to have you executed on sight. However, for now, you are my guest."

She whispered to the guard who untied me and then she left. A guard remained inside the tent with me and I could see silhouettes of at least two more guards outside. For the moment I decided there was nothing to do but enjoy the barbarian hospitality.

14.

THE DAYS PASSED UNEVENTFULLY. I was never let out of my deerskin prison, eating my meals, tending to personal matters, sleeping, and nothing much else for five or six days. I tried talking with my guards, but they spoke a Germanic dialect that was completely foreign to me. I assumed their petite leader had been captured at a fairly young age and, by some strange quirk, had become their champion. I thought it would be quite enlightening to have more of a conversation with the "boss," but she didn't make another appearance.

It was on about the sixth day of my captivity that it happened. I was awakened by loud whooping and shouting, and all the guards suddenly got up and raced away. I stuck my head out of the tent and saw my Roman troops battling my barbarian captors. I was in a bit of a quandary as to what I should do. I assumed they were mounting a rescue attack, although I wasn't really sure why they bothered. I certainly was no asset on the battle field. The only Roman soldier that seemed to care at all about me was Flavius, who I saw in the forefront of the battle. He was putting down Germanic barbarians one after another in a very workmanlike manner. I also saw Augustus doing his part and even Mobus was there, although he was keeping well to the rear. I didn't see the "boss," but I was sure she wasn't far away.

The fighting was getting pretty thick and then it dawned on me: Why was everyone fighting in the first place? What was the point? The Roman soldiers didn't want to be there; they were all outcasts from society. The Germans were no threat at that time. I stood up on a large rock and let out a great roar, louder than anyone could possibly expect, loud enough to startle everyone and make them stop their silly fighting.

"Listen to me, all of you," I began. "What's all this fighting about anyway?" Not very eloquent, but it got my point across. "Can't we settle our differences in some other way? We don't need to annihilate each other. Let's try to be reasonable."

At that moment, the diminutive boss approached.

"What are you saying, Minotaur? We should all just hug each other and forget everything?"

"Why not?" I asked.

Augustus came forward. "It's not the Roman way. We've always fought and taken what we've wanted."

"And we have the right to defend ourselves against Roman tyranny," the boss answered. "But I have a proposal. You and I, we are the leaders of each army; let's you and I fight. Should I win, you and your troops will withdraw, go back to Rome and leave our land to us. If you win, we will cede these lands to Rome and become your subjects. What do you say, Augustus, are these conditions satisfactory?"

Augustus was silent for a moment. He did not have the authority to defy the Senate's orders, but it seemed like a simple way to victory. After all, his opponent seemed less than formidable. He did wonder how his adversary knew his name.

"I accept," he answered.

Each army withdrew to opposite sides of the camp while the "arena," which was a circular enclosure outlined by tree branches, was made ready. The Romans were all smiles, thinking that the duel was already won. Even with one hand Augustus was a skilled, clever and fierce combatant. I however, had the sense that there was something afoot; that the barbarians had a trick that would give them the advantage. It was only a few minutes later that we all found out what it was.

Augustus appeared first, resplendent in his Roman uniform, armor, and red-plumed helmet. His shield was, as always, strapped to his forearm, his broad sword was sheathed along with his long, curved, razor-sharp knife. He carried a spear, which he firmly planted in the ground at one end of the makeshift arena. A few moments later, the boss appeared, her head completely covered, and only her eyes could be seen. Her shield was strapped to her back, and her sword and knife were sheathed. She didn't carry a spear. Two lieutenants met in the middle, spoke briefly, and turned to the gathered troops. Then they spoke, one in Latin, the other in Germanic.

"This is a fight to the death. Each contestant will be allowed their shield, sword, and knife. Let the battle begin."

The two slowly approached each other and met in the center, warily circling around, each holding their sword, seemingly afraid to strike the first blow. Finally, Augustus made the first lunge, thrusting his sword straight towards his adversary's heart. She deftly sidestepped and brought her sword down towards his shoulder in swift retaliation, her move deftly blocked by his shield. The boss's footwork was dazzling as she danced around the arena, demonstrating all the moves that Augustus had never been able to teach me. It was at that moment it hit me; not only did the boss look Roman, she fought like a Roman. As a matter of fact, she fought just like Augustus. She stayed the aggressor, having the advantage of two good hands. She thrust and parried with both her sword and knife, keeping her shield strapped to her back. It was all Augustus could do to keep her at bay, but one time she was careless and Augustus tripped her and she fell to the ground. He pounced on her, attempting to finish it right there, but she rolled away just in time to avoid the sword that was aimed at her throat. She gave him a good kick in the shins and managed to get back on her feet.

It was at this point when the excitement began. The boss ripped off her helmet, displaying her long black hair and dark Roman eyes. Augustus stopped in mid-attack and just stood there.

"You!" he said loudly, his voice full of surprise. "I thought you were long dead."

"I'm still among the living, no thanks to you. Of course, *she* died long ago, of a broken heart," she answered, her voice filled with contempt. She lunged at him with her sword and put a nasty gash in his shoulder, still he didn't move.

"Don't you think I searched high and low? Do you really think I didn't care? Do you think I still don't care?"

"I think—no, I know—that you left us; abandoned us to be with your precious men."

"I had no choice, can't you see. If I'd left them, hundreds would have died. I thought you were safe. I went back as soon as I was able."

"Lies, just lies. You wanted us gone. You only wanted Tobius back. You couldn't stand that your son was gone and all that was left was a worthless daughter. Well, I'm not so worthless now, am I? Are you proud of me, Father? Did I learn all the lessons that you never taught me?"

She lunged at him again and a large chunk of flesh flew off his right flank. Still, he made no move to defend himself. He only stared at her, his face almost beaming with what I assumed to be fatherly pride. His daughter was the fighter I could never be, a leader of men. Another Joseph in Egypt, showing her adopted people how to survive. He dropped his weapons and stood straight up with his arms out as she lunged one more time. The blade pierced his chest and he slumped to the ground.

At first she stood over him, a look of triumph on her face and then she slumped over his lifeless body and whispered something in his ear and started to cry as she wrapped her arms around him.

The whole scene left me nothing but confused. The rest of the company seemed to be just as conflicted, not really sure what they had witnessed. It was at this point that Mobus burst out of whatever hole he had been hiding in.

He yelled, "For Caesar!" and plunged his dagger into the side of the boss. She turned to look at him, only surprise on her face, no pain, and finally, a look of peace as she fell on her father's body, the two joined together in death.

Not the best way to reunite a family, I thought.

Mobus stood up, his look of triumph was short lived as both Romans and Germans descended upon him. It wasn't long before he was nothing but a bloody, lifeless pulp. After this, both sides lost all interest in fighting. The Romans kept their end of the bargain and withdrew. The Germans solemnly celebrated a bittersweet victory. As for me, the whole episode left a sour taste in my mouth. Once again, I'd had enough of humanity and decided to go away. I said my good-byes to Flavius, who was adopted into the German tribe and did not suffer his demise in those barbarous lands, and I headed north, away from fighting, away from people. All I wanted was some time of solitude.

I got a bit more than I bargained for.

15.

I AVOIDED ANY CONTACT WITH people as I journeyed through what are now the Scandinavian countries. The air became chillier, the wind had a bite, and snow and ice covered the land. I ignored the cold as I trudged along ice floes and over glaciers. I had a few brief encounters with reindeer and a distempered polar bear, but otherwise it was just me and snow and ice. I trekked along with no particular plan, occasionally thinking that the Labyrinth wasn't such a bad place, when Fate must have heard my thoughts. I was crossing one of the many glaciers, jumping a deep crevice, when I slipped. Instead of landing safely on the opposite side I fell into the deep hole and found myself wedged between two sheer walls of ice about a hundred feet from the top.

I couldn't go up or down; in fact, I couldn't move at all. I was stuck and it wasn't long before I was frozen. I don't know why I didn't meet my end, but the gods above sometimes play cruel jokes. There I was, stuck upside down and soon I was buried under snow and ice, frozen but still conscious on some level. I guess I was in hibernation. It was as if I was asleep, most of the time oblivious to everything, but sometimes having vivid and bizarre dreams. For all practical purpose I was back in the Labyrinth, trapped with little hope for release. I clearly remember thinking that nature had played a very cruel joke, locking me away in a living death of frozen oblivion.

It was the dreams that were my only source of hope; nightmares or fantasies or tender, sweet thoughts that seemed to come to life, they all helped me keep a sense of sanity. And some of them were quite fantastic:

I was back in the old Labyrinth, except it was very different. The hedge was still high, but there were no razor-sharp thorns, and no "sacrifices" every year. This Labyrinth was a place so beautiful I never wanted to leave. Fragrant flowers of every possible color adorned the hedge and the branches were laden with fine fruit—pomegranates, apples, and vines bearing plump grapes. It was warm and sunny and a great sense of peace filled my soul.

This must be Heaven, I remember thinking, and I wanted the feeling to go on forever. I heard footsteps running towards me and then panting. A man approached, out of breath, but the footsteps quickened. I anxiously awaited the arrival of some sort of wonderful being, a god or angel of god. Imagine my disappointment when the footsteps slowed and that reprobate, Theseus, entered my dream. Not what I had hoped for.

"Hurry, she needs our help," he panted as he pressed his hands to his knees trying to catch his breath. "Follow me and I'll show you the way."

I wasn't sure if I should trust him. The Theseus I knew was much more scoundrel than hero and besides, that place seemed so wonderful, I didn't want to leave.

"Come on," he said, "I can't save her by myself. Orpheus is doing all he can, but he's getting tired and if he stops playing, well, she'll be done for I'm sure."

I shook my head as if to empty it of cobwebs and asked, "Who'll be done for?"

"Eurydice, you dumb bull. She's being held by Hades and he won't release her, even though we paid the price."

"What can I do?" I asked, looking around at my beautiful Labyrinth with a sense of longing in my heart.

"You're the Minotaur, stupid. Everyone is afraid of you. Even the gods are afraid of you. I'm the only one that's not afraid because I know what a big fraud you are. Now hurry and try to act just a little ferocious."

I still wasn't sure about the whole scenario, and I was sure that I was just dreaming, but he seemed so real and I didn't have anything else to do, so I was off with him. We only went a short distance when everything, all the beauty and wonder that had surrounded me faded away, replaced by darkness and fire and screeching noises. The Underworld, Hades domain, a place of eternal torture. The only good thing was the sweet sound of Orpheus's singing and the lyre he played. He sang about Eros and Psyche, a sad song of betrayal and lost love.

I saw a woman, Eurydice, I presumed, seated at the bottom of a hill, held captive, encircled by thick vines that seemed to have reached out from the ground and grabbed her. At the top of the hill sat the dark Lord, Hades, and his consort, Persephone. She was entranced by the beautiful, soulful sounds that Orpheus produced, but Hades only glared, his eyes ablaze.

As the singing grew louder all of the underworld stopped to listen. Tantalus forgot his thirst and Sisyphus paused in his task of rolling the large boulder. Shades and ghosts stopped in midair as Orpheus moved on from Eros and Psyche to Theseus and the Minotaur.

"That's our cue," whispered Theseus. "Let's go."

At that point I wasn't sure what was going on, but after a few moments my role became obvious. Theseus drew his sword and attacked me and I fought back, more fiercely than I had ever fought before (it was only a dream, after all). As we fought we moved closer and closer to Eurydice and to Hades. Orpheus kept up his riveting music as all the Underworld became distracted by the commotion. By this time, Theseus and

I were right on top of Eurydice and, at that moment, Theseus gave me a quick push towards Hades and Persephone, while he gave a few sharp whacks with his sword, freeing Eurydice from her bonds. Hades stood up quickly, his eyes glowing a bright red and he grew to Titan size as Theseus, Orpheus, and Eurydice started to race away. The lord of the Underworld reached out with his now giant hand and tried to corral the escaping heroes. He found his way blocked by, of all things, me. I had grown to a size even larger than Hades and I grabbed his arm in my hand and twisted it around his back.

The three escapees jumped into Charon's boat, threw him three pennies, and seemed to make their escape. I was left alone, battling Hades and his minions. The moment Theseus, Orpheus, and Eurydice vanished from sight, the dream ceased and I found myself awake, numb and surrounded by white, back in the Labyrinth. The dream left me a bit unsettled, not knowing how it ended or what it all meant. I wondered what happened between Theseus and Orpheus. Knowing what I knew about Theseus, I assumed he would try to seduce the girl, have his way, and then leave her to Orpheus. But I also remembered the real story of Orpheus in the Underworld, in which case Eurydice would not have made it out and everything would have been for nothing. I sort of leaned towards the latter, but it really was moot. It was, after all, only a dream.

16.

MY DREAMS DEPARTED FROM GREEK lore and moved on to Egypt, specifically to Moses who was tending his father-in-law's herds in the land of Midian. He was already married and was content to be settled in his mundane life when he saw the burning bush. This is where the drama really began. As Moses made his way towards the burning bush he met a man. There was nothing very distinctive about this man, except he was dressed in an unusual manner, what I now realize was modern twenty-first century garb, rather than the robes and sandals of that time. He was short with fair skin wearing a black coat, blue jeans, and a black top hat. This man stopped Moses before he could approach God, who was within that burning bush. The man spoke, a melodious voice that mesmerized the listener.

"Don't go any further," the man said. "That bush is dangerous. It will take you away from your family and increase your burden a hundredfold. Listen to me if you know what's good for you. I can give you so much more. If you follow me I will increase your flocks a hundredfold and give you many sons."

"How can you do this?" Moses asked, seeming to be tempted by the offer. "Are you a god?"

"I am more than a god, Moses. I am given charge over all that happens in this world. I can give you riches beyond your wildest dreams. I can make you Pharaoh, give you a hundred wives."

"You are just a man, like me," Moses answered.

"Can a mere man do this?" the other responded.

The other man picked up a stone, waved his hand, and the rock became pure gold. It was at this moment that I appeared in the dream, in completely bovine form—a *vicious* bull. I snorted and pawed at the ground, making my presence known. And, although I was pure bull, if you'll pardon my expression, I still had the consciousness of a man. At that moment I knew that the fate of mankind rested upon Moses resisting his tempter and proceeding forward to approach and address God in the burning bush.

I didn't have many options; therefore, I charged the two of them in my best bull-like fashion. Moses easily sidestepped my assault, but his adversary was not so lucky. I threw that demon over my head and he landed on the ground with a thud about ten meters away. He didn't move immediately and Moses stared at him and then the burning bush and then back at that "man." Without further hesitation he took steps toward the burning bush and, when that demonic being saw what had happened he let out a great howl, louder than any wolf ever howled. His eyes burned red, filled with fire, as he stared at me with hatred. He stood straight up and gestured and we both disappeared. Moses, having entered the holy ground of God, was protected, but I found myself back in my old form surrounded by fire and the smell of burning sulfur. I realized at that point that if I hadn't intervened, Moses never would have been chosen by God to lead the Israelites out of Egypt and the world may have turned out to be a much different place. Of course, it was only a dream. I woke up and found myself back in my white, icy prison, the now familiar and frigid, but in this instance, comforting, Labyrinth.

17.

TIME CAME TO A STANDSTILL for me during that period of imprisonment. It was as if I was in conscious hibernation. I really should have died, but for some reason, the powers above kept me alive, as if there was some purpose for me in the time to come. I remember one other vivid dream from that time.

I was back in the ancient holy land; during the time of false prophets and Messiahs, a new one popping up every week, it seemed. I was completely human for once and I remember I was strolling through what seemed to be a bazaar. There were people at tables changing money, selling various types of animals along with a variety of other goods. That place was bustling with commerce and most everyone seemed happy. However, after strolling a short ways I heard shouting at the end of the courtyard.

"...den of thieves," a man shouted and then I heard tables being upended.

I ran to see what all the commotion was, but it seemed to end almost as soon as it started. The angry man was very familiar; he was the same man that rescued me from that sealed cave, this man called Jesus.

The dream jumped ahead to another time, some days or weeks later, I guessed. There was an eerily familiar gathering of people along the streets of Jerusalem, staring into the streets at a processional, some sort of parade. I looked into the street and saw the same man, beaten and bloody carrying a heavy wooden cross, just as I'd seen him years before. Two others were also carrying crosses, but they had not suffered the same type of beating that Jesus had suffered. As they passed by, Jesus stumbled and the weight of the cross fell on top of him and it seemed he couldn't get up. I ran out, with a few other men, and we lifted the cross off his bloody back and I helped him to his feet. One of the Roman guards commanded me to carry the cross, which I gladly did.

As we walked, I spoke with this man.

"Lord," I said (I'm not sure why I called him "Lord"), "why are they treating you with such hatred? Is it because you upset the bazaar? That seems to be such a minor offense, certainly not deserving of such severe punishment."

He gave me a half smile, but said nothing. I looked at the guard standing next to me and I noticed his face was very familiar. It was the same face I'd seen trying to stop Moses in the last dream, the same actor that had appeared in desert, the face of every spectator that had witnessed Jesus' execution before. *That is an evil man*, I thought. *Surely I can stop this travesty of justice. All I have to do is stop that man and I can save Jesus. Just a little swing of this heavy cross, open a path through the crowd, and we can be gone.*

I looked ahead for a good getaway spot and then Jesus spoke, only one word, but it carried incredible power.

"No."

It was as if He'd read my every thought and at that moment I knew that all that was happening, all His suffering, was for the best. Evil thought it was about to triumph, but in reality it was about to be vanquished forever. I carried the cross the rest of the way and then they sent me away. I watched the Evil One drive the nails through His hands and feet and hang Him up to die. When He had breathed His last breath and His head slumped, I woke up, back in my frozen prison. I thought about Him suffering on the Cross, but also about the cave, the light, and the stone being pushed away. At that very moment I felt some shaking and movement and then more movement. The ice that held me captive slipped and slid and then fell with a crash into the sea. I was still prisoner, but I was out of the Labyrinth once again, as this newly created iceberg floated out to sea.

The iceberg bobbed up and down with the waves, churning my long empty stomach as my head started to spin with each spasm of nausea. My icy prison started to melt and more and more light reached my eyes. I sensed I was coming closer and closer to freedom. Now I could see fish occasionally swim past and the spout of whales washed the front of my frozen window from time to time. Luckily, I was right at the water line; I initially worried that I would have my head free from ice underwater and would drown if my feet were still imprisoned, but now I figured I'd be safe above water. Nausea still plagued me from time to time, but I finally was becoming accustomed to the rhythmic bobbing.

Finally, the ice melted enough so that my nose was free. The smell of salt air filled my nostrils with my first real breath in eons and I heard the calls of sea gulls giving me hope that land was not far away. Soon my whole head was free and then neck, shoulders, arms, trunk, hips, feet, and toes. I just pushed away and paddled after the gulls. Land wasn't far off. I wondered what I would find, but, even more, I wondered when, because I had no idea how long I'd been held captive. I washed up on the shore of what would now be Normandy, France. An invasion of one; D-Day, at least for me.

18.

I MADE MY WAY TO the beach of Normandy and lay in the sand, caressed by the warm sun. Years, actually centuries, melted away as my old bones and joints basked in the warm glow and started to loosen. I fell asleep staring up at the blue sky, thankful for my new freedom and totally uncaring about where I was or what the future would bring. My carefree attitude was short-lived, however. I woke up far from the beach, in the back of a wagon, drawn by an old horse and driven by an elderly man dressed in strange clothes.

"Excuse me, sir," I said as politely as I could, in Latin, then Greek and, finally, the German dialect.

He turned his head and smiled, but didn't speak as he drove on, past fields and forest. The road was rough, pocked with muddy holes and rocks. The horse moved along at a pretty good clip which made for a very bumpy ride.

"Can you tell me where I am?" I asked in Latin.

This time he answered, speaking rapidly in a language that seemed to have some remnants of Latin, enough so that I could make out that he was taking me to the castle and they were all waiting for me. This left me more than a little confused, but, after being incommunicado for such a long time I was ready to get back into any world that would accept me.

After two days of travel I finally saw the tall towers and garrets in the distance as we winded our way over the rough, narrow road. Dense forest surrounded the trail allowing only a trickle of sunlight to reach us. My driver became more loquacious as we came closer to the castle and I quickly picked up the dialect, a cross between ancient Latin and modern French.

"My name is Jacques," he told me. "Jacques Dumbe, the royal driver, at your service. Our old King was completely inadequate and we had to send him away. You will do much better, I'm sure."

I wasn't exactly sure what he meant by "sent away" or how I would "do much better," but I was in no position to argue at that moment.

We entered a ravine and the spires of the castle vanished behind the trees.

"Only a short distance to go," my cheerful driver announced. "Maurice will be so ecstatic when he sees you. We'll finally show up those clowns over in Lovia. They think their prince is so special, wait until they see our King!"

I thought for a moment and then asked, "Jacques, what makes you think I should be King? You don't know anything about me really. I suppose I should be grateful, but I'd like to know how you found me and where we are going."

"It was the prophecy, of course. How else would we have known about you? The prophet, Topaz, in the year 1158 spoke of a great leader who would come from the sea and here you are."

"What year is it now?" I asked.

"Why, it's 1329," he replied.

"How did you know I'd come at this time. It seems your prophecy was a long time ago."

"Oh, Topaz's prophecies always come true, sooner or later. There was the time we had the drought, four years, and no more than a thimble full of rain. Well, we were in desperate straits, as I'm sure you can fathom. But, he prophesied rain and, sure enough, it came. It only took fourteen months that time, but, oh, how it rained, days and days, weeks and weeks, until everything was washed away. And, after that he predicted that there would be flies and disease and he was right again. Hundreds died from the blight. We had no King at that time, no one divinely placed to appeal to God. And now, here you are, a new King," he said, his voice becoming choked up with emotion.

"One more question, if you don't mind," I responded. "How did you know when I'd be coming?"

"Oh, we didn't really know. That beach is the only part of Etouffe that borders the Great Sea. We've had a sentry stationed there since Topaz's great prophecy. When you emerged from the waters they sounded the alert and one of our swift riders brought notice to the palace. And now, here we are. Our last two Kings also came from the sea, but, alas, they weren't very regal. They both had to go. But, you... I just know you're the real King. Why just look at you, the head of a bull. What could be more kingly than that?"

This could be trouble, I thought. We traveled on in silence after that.

We finally reached the bottom of the ravine and as we started up the opposite side I heard an unusual noise, a bird call, but artificial. A few moments later there was some loud whooping and then a loud whinny from the horse. An arrow flew out of the woods and lodged in the wagon only a couple of inches from my hand.

"Bandits," whispered Jacques. "Don't worry. They won't dare rob the new King."

Not much to rob was all I could think as a band of about ten men on horseback surrounded us. One who seemed to be the leader rode up to me, brandishing his sword.

"I heard there was a new King coming. More like a new freak, if you ask me. Tell me, Jacques, are you digging up your kings from the dung heaps now?" he asked, dropping his sword a bit as he addressed my driver.

"You'll get lost, Pierre, if you know what's good for you. This King is straight from God and will rid the land of scum like you," Jacques answered, with more defiance than I expected.

Might as well play my part. I don't want to find out what they'll do when they learn there's nothing of value here. I stood up in the back of the wagon and let out a roar. Actually, it felt pretty good to clear out my lungs after all that time. There were some old rotting planks of wood in the cart and I gathered one up and swung it back and forth, catching one of the bandits across the chest, and knocking him to the ground. This was enough to startle Pierre, who dropped his guard long enough for me to grab his wrist and shake his sword free. *Not much of thief,* I thought as I picked him up by one arm, gave him a brief sneer and a smile (which probably looked like even more of a sneer), and threw him to the ground.

"Some thief," I hissed, nothing but loathing in my voice. "Next time, you should think twice before tangling with the Minotaur. I've battled far worse than the likes of you, you pitiful little wretch. Now, leave my kingdom and, if I ever catch you in these parts again, you'll get a taste of my sword. Now go."

And I spat at the ground and signaled for Jacques to drive on before our adversaries had time to regroup. He took off at a swift gallop and we reached the castle after a few more hours. *I guess I've passed the test so far,* I thought, but I was worried I'd see Pierre or something worse. Although Pierre apparently heeded my warning, what I did eventually encounter was definitely much worse.

19.

A LONG LINE OF STAFF lined up to greet me and be inspected. At one end was a man who seemed to be in charge of all the rest. I soon learned that he was Maurice, the head butler. He approached me first while the others stood quietly in a line. I told Maurice I wasn't ready to review the "troops"; I needed to get cleaned up and to put on some proper clothes. He dismissed them all with a wave of his gloved hand and escorted me to my chambers.

"Welcome, welcome your Majesty." He sniffed in a condescending tone. "If anything can be done to make your reign more comfortable, please call on me and my staff at any time. We are only here to serve you and attend to your every need and desire. In your chambers you will find suitable attire, your royal robe and crown, and Monsieur Rollo, your valet. He will help you clean up and dress. If you should need anything from me, pull any one of these laced cords that are found around the castle. I will respond immediately. Here is your room. I will withdraw now to see that dinner is properly prepared. Dinner is served promptly at seven. Good day, your Majesty."

I walked through the massive doorway into a spacious room that was as opulent as could be found in those times. There was a huge canopy bed stacked with fine woven blankets as well as furs.

"We have some new clothes for you, your Majesty. I didn't get your unusual measurements until yesterday, but my staff and I have managed to create a few special items for you to wear. Here is a fine day coat for you and a linen robe fringed with fine silk. May I help you dress?"

I took off the ragged coat I was wearing and Rollo let out a loud "Gasp!"

"Does my appearance frighten you, Rollo? I'm sorry."

"It's not your bullish figure, sir. It's just that you are so disheveled and worn. May I help you clean up and perhaps, appear a bit more, shall we say, kingly?"

I looked in the mirror and saw what poor Rollo saw. My horns were chipped and cracked, my neck was thin and wasted, my eyes were sunken, my ribs stuck out, and my legs were bony toothpicks. To make things worse, my skin was covered with sores and abrasions.

"You are certainly free to do what you will. Anything would be an improvement," I observed.

Rollo pulled on one of the silken cords and in a few moments I heard water being poured, footsteps running here and there, and then one of the servants appeared with a large, cushioned chair and they carried me into the bath where I received a hot bath, scrubbed from horn to toe, sores dressed with a balm that soothed and, almost miraculously, healed. I was dressed in a fine silk robe and then they brought a sumptuous meal, my first food in over a thousand years, washed down with a fine red wine. After this excellent meal, Maurice met me and I was introduced to the staff, the first in a series of introductions that I was to experience over the next few days.

In rapid fire, Maurice reeled off the names of the hired help: Lemuel, the cook; Afghan, the cook's assistant; Alton, the pastry chef; Anton, the dishwasher; Memeon, the butler's assistant; Yvette, the upstairs maid; Evette, the downstairs maid; Rollo, the valet; Francoise, the valet's assistant; Boulet, the shoe shiner; Ed, the horse trainer; Lemaire, the stable boy; and about a dozen others I can't remember.

Each gave a proper bow or curtsy and swore their undying allegiance to me and then went back to work. I started to ask Maurice about the previous Kings and if the staff had also sworn their "undying allegiance to *them*," but he cut me off.

"You shall be the finest King we've ever known, your royal Highness, I'm certain," he stated. I was sure he'd spoken the exact words many times before.

I spent the rest of that night and the next day wandering about the grounds, inspecting the flower gardens, the stables, the ponds, and lakes. The huntsman, Rafael, showed me his latest "kill," a wild boar which would be the evening meal.

At dinner time I sat down alone to a banquet with enough food for twenty. The main dining room had a table thirty feet long. The walls were adorned with fine tapestries showing scenes of war and councils and marriages; presumably all important events in the history of Etouffe. I ate a hearty meal of fruits and bread, drank some more fine wine, and then settled in front of the huge fire. Logs the size of tree trunks burned in a fireplace that was at least forty feet across. After centuries in the deep freeze, I was grateful for the fire's warmth and lingered in front of it for the rest of the night.

I was roused out of sleep by Rollo in the early morning hours, holding a candle and carrying a basin of water.

"What time is it?" I asked, shaking the cobwebs out of my head and stretching my arms.

"About three a.m., your Royal Highness. Your presence is needed in the servant's quarters, a big ruckus between Lemaire and Francoise."

"What's that got to do with me?" I asked naively. "Oh yeah, I'm the King, I forgot. Well, show me the way."

After a quick pit stop, Rollo led me to the servants' quarters at the far end of the castle. It must have been about a quarter of a mile walk. There I found Lemaire holding a knife and Francoise holding a bloody rag against his side. Memeon and Anton were holding Lemaire, who was arguing with Francoise in rapid fire French. Evette (or was it Yvette?) was sitting nearby, wrapped in Maurice's robe, I assumed, as it was adorned with a large "M" and was fairly elaborate. I quickly surmised what had happened, but as King, I was supposed to investigate and render some sort of judgment.

"OK," I began, "tell me what happened, Msr. Lemaire or Francoise. I don't care who begins." I stole a quick glance at the lovely Evette who sat on one of the mats with her head down.

Lemaire began to speak, "That cheat. Who does he think he is, stealing my valuable possession?"

"What did he steal?" I queried, trying to sound official.

"Look in his hand and you'll see."

I did notice that Francoise was clutching a chain in his left hand.

"I won this fair and square, your Majesty, just ask the others."

"Open your hand, Francoise, let me see what all the fuss and bloodshed is about."

He opened his hand and revealed gold chain with a star-shaped diamond-encrusted pendant.

I turned to Memeon and Anton. "What can you tell me about this?"

They looked at each other and then at me, and finally Anton spoke.

"I did see them rolling dice, your Highness, but I don't know nothing more."

Memeon added, "It's *her* fault, your Majesty. She wanted that necklace for herself. They were cheating poor Lemaire, sir.

"Liar!" screamed Evette and she lunged at Memeon and scratched him across the face before Rollo pulled her away.

"Do you have something to add, Ms. Evette?" I asked, thinking that I sounded like a kindergarten teacher. Perhaps that was appropriate, seeing how the entire bunch was acting like little children. She sat silently, pouting and refusing to speak.

"I will take that necklace for now. Until I can learn the truth I will keep this in safekeeping. Now, all of you, back to bed, except Francoise. You come with me and we'll see about getting you patched up."

I brought Francoise up to my room where I found a needle and some thread. I had Rollo clean the wound with soap and hot water. I took the needle and thread and sewed that gash closed. I had seen the Romans do something similar after battles. See one, do one, I figured. I sat back to admire my handiwork, applied some clean bandages, which I wrapped firmly around Francoise's waist, and sent him back to his quarters. Before he left, however, I took the dice he had been clutching in his hand, just to check things out as part of my investigation.

After he'd left I studied that gold necklace and particularly the pendant under the pale light of the fire. It was a dazzling bit of artistry, polished and sparkling as if it came straight from Tiffany, adorned with a finely detailed, carved image. I also examined the dice and discovered that they were loaded; Francoise had been cheating Lemaire. I shoved the chain and pendant in my pocket and lay down on the bed, hoping that wisdom and discernment would somehow be planted in my brain in the next few hours.

No revelation came to me and I pretended the entire affair never happened. I gave the jeweled necklace back to Lemaire, told Maurice I didn't want to be bothered with such trivia anymore, and spent the rest of that day in my room, seeing only Rollo. It felt like a black cloud descended and covered me with gloom. Perhaps it was the culmination of a thousand years of solitude; maybe it was the petty tribulations that confront humanity every day. I became a sullen, morose, reclusive

King and nothing anyone did or said, nothing I did or tried to do, brought me any release. I couldn't sleep, but stayed in bed not caring to bathe or eat. There's no doubt that I had entered a deep depression, desperately in need of Prozac.

20.

I T WAS A FEW MONTHS after I'd descended into this funk and turned all of the decision making duties over to Rollo that she came. I'd become more or less a recluse, staying in the castle, rarely venturing outside my room. I couldn't deal with the responsibilities that being King demanded and seeing any people upset me tremendously. I became an angry, miserable, depressed beast; even the servants avoided me, all except Rollo. He became my trusted confidante, a truly remarkable man who only had other peoples' best interests in his heart.

Anyway, back to her, Clarice, a young beauty who wandered into my life one day. Well, wandered isn't the right term. No she showed up at the castle door one evening and started pounding away, screaming something about men chasing her and her horse breaking down and I don't know what else. Anyway, Maurice let her in, gave her a fine meal, and a room to sleep in. Lemaire and Francoise searched the grounds and surrounding areas, but no men were found and her horse pranced around like a young pony, never taking a bad step.

But, she was there and she had no intention of leaving until she'd met the master of the house. At the time, I didn't know if she was running away, deluded, dangerous, or just curious. I'd kept myself locked away for more than five years and, I suppose, there were stories; stories about me, declaring that I was some sort of fearsome monster, a ravenous beast that devoured virgins and stole children in the middle of the night. I assumed she was curious, but she also had to be fearless to come to my supposed castle of horrors, alone, in the middle of the night. I instructed the servants to attend to her needs and to be with her at all times. I was not ready to meet anyone new, particularly a beautiful young maid who almost certainly had ulterior motives.

The first few days of her "visit" were uneventful. She received the finest meals, the upstairs maids attended to her in every way. Fine new clothes sewn from linen and silk were brought to her. She truly received the royal treatment. After all, I hadn't had a visitor in years. Maurice seemed to relish the opportunity to provide service and he kept the staff running to and fro, cooking gourmet meals, polishing every little nook, all the while keeping his ears open. He reported to Rollo who then reported to me. I'm sure that deep down the entire staff hoped that this Clarice would free me from the melancholy that had bewitched me. In the end she did, but not in the way anyone expected.

Of course, my curiosity overcame my depression and I started to spy on her. It was nothing lurid or unseemly. Surely after all I've told you so far you wouldn't think me capable of ungentlemanly behavior. I watched her dine and walk about the grounds. She would sing in a very sweet and lilting soprano voice as she walked along, joyful songs of love and springtime, sad songs of lost love and fading romance. Each note was more enchanting than the last and I was fast becoming captivated by her. After several weeks, I made plans to meet her.

It was to be after dinner, a time she would sit by the fire in the large parlor and draw images of angels among the clouds, animals in the forest, and anything else that tickled her fancy. She was quite an accomplished artist. She sketched in charcoal first and then colored with some oily markers that she found in one of the closets, bold bright colors mixed with soft pastels. This painting on the stand behind me is her portrait of me, pretty good I'd say, although I was a bit heavier in those days, all that fine French cooking.

The big day finally came; I'd mustered up the courage to introduce myself and Rollo was making sure I looked the part. His crew scrubbed me from horn to toenail. Polished what could be polished, shampooed, styled and coiffed every hair, dressed me in the finest suit and, the final touch, gave me a single golden rose to present to the lovely lady. I skipped dinner, I was so nervous, just like a pimply-faced teenager on his way to pick up his equally awkward date for the junior prom.

That evening I assumed everything was ready. She had finished her dinner and, I was told, was settled in the parlor. I had planned a big entrance, accompanied by a Maurice on the violin. The music preceded me through the double doors and then I made my grand entrance, greeted by an empty room. Needless to say I was a bit perturbed.

"Where is she?" I screamed and waved my arms, smacking poor Maurice across the chin and splintering his violin into a million toothpicks. "Where is she?" I screamed even louder, throwing the flower to the ground. It was at this moment, after I'd ruined any hint of romantic atmosphere, rumpled every inch of my suit, and spilled red wine on my horns and feet that the lady reappeared. She took a look at me and the disaster of a parlor and then looked back at me and started to laugh. At first I wanted to run and hide, and send her away, but then I looked at myself in the mirror. My horns had purple blotches on them and there was a tapestry hanging from my right horn. My perfectly-pressed black suit was rumpled and two buttons were missing. There were bits of wood everywhere and purple blotches on my white shirt and shoes. I have to admit I was a pretty comical sight. I started to laugh and soon everyone had a big laugh. Clarice took her seat by the fire and I sat opposite her, while Rollo appeared and started to clean my horns.

At this moment Clarice jumped up and took the polishing cloth from Rollo and started to clean my horns. It's a good thing that I have black fir instead of skin, because I was plenty embarrassed. I know she didn't realize it, but cleaning horns is a very intimate act in bovine culture. But, I let her do it. It had been a long time since a member of the opposite sex, human or bovine, had polished my horns. From that moment onward, she was the center of my life.

We entered a period of romantic interlude which, in modern cinema, would be depicted as laughing together while riding on horseback, sitting by the fire holding hands, walking along the beach illuminated by a vivid sunset, and every other cliché one can imagine. It was all that and more. She told me stories of her family, a sister married to a prince, a father who was off traveling most of the time, her mother who would sit by the window of their small home every night and stare into the eastern horizon until night lowered its black quilt. I, on the other hand, dazzled her with stories of Pharaohs, Greek heroes, African Queens, and Roman warriors.

She would sit and listen intently, her head resting on her hands, but always with a perplexed look on her face. I asked her about it one day.

"Clarice, my dear, why do you look so glum? Have I displeased you in any way?"

She would look up and smile and always answer, "Of course not; I've never been happier."

Her words said this, but her eyes revealed a sadness and worry that I was determined to erase and replace with nothing but joy and happiness.

Over the weeks I tried everything. Extraordinary, fancy meals with the finest venison, truffled pastas, the freshest vegetables, vintage wines, and desserts of the richest pastries and creams were followed by performances by the finest travelling troubadours on the continent. I lavished her with gifts of the most extraordinary, luxurious jewels, finest silk garments. Gradually the look of sadness faded and her eyes were filled with contentment. At that point I confided to Rollo.

"It's time, I think, time to make Clarice a permanent part of my life. What do you think?" I asked my close confidant.

Rollo, rather than agreeing immediately, took a few moments, furrowed his brow, started to speak, and then stopped. He started to again, but still no words came out. I began to feel a bit perplexed and finally, in my exasperation, exclaimed "Well?" in a long slow sarcastic tone.

Finally he answered, "She's a most wonderful girl, and I know that you love her. Are you sure she loves you?"

"Of course she loves me. Haven't I given her everything any woman could ever want? What more could I do?"

Rollo still had a look of worry on his face.

"You know, boss, I would do anything for you. You have given me so much, taught me a great deal, and I am your most devoted servant. I don't want to see you hurt. All your life it's been nothing but hurt for you. I don't mean to be disrespectful, but the sad truth is that you've never quite fit into any world. Not among humans, nor among cows. You've lived thousands of years, but almost all that time you've been trapped, imprisoned by the Labyrinth, either real or imaginary. Do you think Clarice has the key to release you? Or, is it just blind hope on your part?"

Now it was my turn to be silent. Nothing he said was news to me. As a matter of fact, I had thought of all those things before. But it was time to make a stand for myself.

I slammed my fist down on the table.

"She has to love me! She has to!" I wailed. "She's the only chance I've ever had to escape the Labyrinth, even if it's only for short time. Isn't that worth the risk? Isn't one minute of true love worth a thousand lifetimes of sorrow?"

"I don't know," Rollo answered. "I don't know."

I really didn't know either, but I had resolved to try to break free and bring happiness to both of us.

"This is what I have for her," I said to Rollo as I produced a finely burnished, solid wooden box. I slowly, dramatically opened the lid, revealing a golden crown, encrusted with diamonds and rubies, and a ring, adorned with the likeness of a bull and encrusted with the finest diamonds.

"Very impressive," Rollo stated. "She'll love them. I don't suppose you've given any thought to the age difference. Let's see, you're almost three thousand and she's, what, maybe seventeen?"

I smiled at his comment. "I believe the species differential is a bit more of a hurdle than the May December aspect."

We both laughed out loud, hiding the worry that each of us felt.

21.

I DIDN'T SLEEP AT ALL that night, tossing and turning and, finally, getting up out of bed to sit by the window. I stared out into the clear, dark night and looked up at the sliver of moon that provided faint illumination. So many questions filled my head.

Was this to be the culmination of my life?

Had the gods kept me around for this purpose—to be a mate to this lovely young lady?

Could she really love me, a hideous, but sensitive freak?

Would I continue to live on forever while she aged and died?

The last question filled me with despair and I wondered if I was being selfish. Who was I? Why should I bring this innocent girl into my life? Didn't she deserve something better?

For the last time in my life, I knelt down and prayed. I prayed, once again, to every god I'd ever known: African, Greek, Roman, Egyptian, Hebrew, Christian; they were all the same to me and if just one of them was real, he or she would hear.

"Dear gods,

"I know I am nothing to you, an insignificant being, but you've kept me alive for all these years for a reason. Please, help me to understand, to know that a life with this sweet girl is why I have lived this long life. Help me to show her all the love I feel in my heart and make us happy together. Grant me the courage to show her and tell her of my undying love."

I finished this prayer and looked up at the dark night sky. The moon was gone, hidden by clouds and then there was a flash and the loud CRACK of thunder.

An answer to prayer, I surmised, but what did the answer mean? A resounding YES or a warning? I went back to my bed, more confused, but also ready for the big day.

The storm lasted through the night, but the dawn brought bright, warm sunshine. I had breakfast in my room with Rollo, alfalfa sprouts, dandelion and rolled oats. The morning was spent cleaning me up and, finally, I was ready to meet her. A late morning walk through the Rose Garden promised the perfect setting for romantic confessions. We met at the entrance and I took her petite hand in mine.

With a wavering voice I started my well-rehearsed speech:

"H-Have you been happy here, Clarice? Do I make you happy? Y-you have so f-filled me with joy, at times I think I'll explode."

She looked at me and then smiled, a tremendous, joyous smile, as if a wonderful realization had just been planted in her brain and her greatest dream fulfilled.

"Why, Miny," she began, "you have been so good to me, lavishing such wonderful gifts and so much attention. You're the most wonderful person I've ever met, man, boy, or beast."

She put her arms around my neck and kissed me on my horn.

I continued, "W-would you be happy spending your life with me? I know I'm different from you, older and horrid, but I love you. With all my heart, I love you."

She ran ahead of me and then stopped to look at my face and then threw her arms around my neck and gave me a big hug and, then, kissed me on my mouth.

"Of course, I love you. You are the kindest, sweetest person I've ever known. I hope that I can spend all of my days with you here in this wonderful castle."

After I heard her confession, needless to say, I was speechless. We just walked along among the roses, holding hands, her head resting on my arm and me with a silly grin on my face. It was the happiest moment of my life, at least up to that time. It was too bad it couldn't last forever.

After a few minutes, she seemed to change, grow restless, as if she was waiting for something. Every few seconds she would look at my face, look up at the sky, and then back to my face. Finally, she spoke, "When's it going to happen?"

At first I was confused, but then I assumed she was referring to our wedding.

"Soon," I answered. "As soon as arrangements can be made. These things take a little time, you know. We have to call the priest, send out invitations, bake a cake, you know, make plans."

She stopped and stared into my eyes. Anger had replaced joy and happiness and her eyes seemed to be filling with disgust.

"I'm not talking about a wedding, Miny. No, I was wondering when you're going to change."

Now I was confused and starting to feel a bit warm.

"Change, my dear? Change in what way?"

"You know, change, from a beast into a prince. Surely you didn't think I could... I mean my sister, that wimpy Belle, confessed her love to a horrid beast and now she's off in a castle, married to the 'enchanted Prince,' and expecting her second child. Well, what about me? I'm twice the woman she is. I confessed my love to an even more hideous beast. Aren't you going to be carried up by 'gossamer wings of light' and revert back into a handsome prince? Isn't the spell broken?"

I stopped and stared into her eyes and then grabbed her shoulders.

"Listen, Clarice," I began, my voice shaking with a mixture of anger and profound disappointment. "This is me, this has always been me. There is no spell. I was born the Minotaur and I'll die the Minotaur. I'm not a handsome noble prince or King trapped in an enchanted, beastly body. I washed up on the shore and was declared King. I'm not royalty; I'm just a beast—part bull, part man. And now, if you can do me the favor, leave me and never come back. You may keep all the gifts. They mean nothing to me."

She stared at me incredulously and then starting beating me with her fists.

"You're a monster! Worse than a beast, an evil monster preying on an innocent girl. No one will ever love you, you hideous, evil..."

She didn't finish her tirade. Rollo had appeared and silenced her. I never saw her, nor heard mention of her again. Every trace of her existence was removed from the castle and I returned to my solitude, a bit wiser and a lot older.

So much for prayer, I thought. Another cruel joke played on me by the gods. I sat in my room and cried. This chapter of my life had mercifully come to an abrupt end.

22.

I REMAINED SECLUDED IN MY room for a few weeks, seeing no one but Rollo. I knew I couldn't stay in that place, facing the daily reminders of my folly, facing the ridicule of the people and even my own servants. Rollo had pretty much been running things for years anyway. So, one night I simply disappeared. I travelled east at first, then south, then further east. I avoided all contact with people, stayed away from roads, blended in with the cows whenever possible. I ended up in what would be Romania today, Transylvania to be exact.

I can see what you're thinking—Transylvania, the legendary home of the fictional Count Dracula. I did meet a rather unusual person there, maybe it was Dracula. Of course I know the legends surrounding the vampire, but the person I met and befriended was Vlad.

I think the year was about 1440 or thereabouts. I came across a castle, dark gray and a bit foreboding, actually. I'd decided to give it a wide berth, avoid it completely as I made my way south towards Greece, perhaps make my way back to Crete, see if the old Labyrinth was still there. It was the whimpering that caught my ear. I wish I'd just ignored it, but my sensitive soul and conscious would not let me.

It was a mongrel puppy, nothing special, tied to a stake, emaciated, its little body covered with sores. It was nighttime and the pitiful creature stood in clearing illuminated by a full moon. I hadn't had a dog in a while; nothing wrong with wanting a bit of unthreatening companionship. I went over to the poor beast and freed her. It was then that he made himself known.

"Hey, leave that dog alone," he shouted. "Now you've gone and spoiled all my sport."

I hadn't noticed anything that resembled any type of sport, just cruelty and torture. He came out of the shadows, a boy, perhaps thirteen, thin and pale in the faint light.

"That's my dog and I'm allowed to do anything that pleases me with it."

"Dogs look to us for help and protection, young man," I scolded.

He came closer, briefly stared at my strange appearance, shrugged his shoulders, and picked up the puppy.

"Your dog looks like he needs some attention and kindness, not torture in the moonlight," I added.

"Here," he said, handing the dog to me. "You feel so sorry for it, it's yours. It looks like the two of you are made for each other."

He started to laugh and I realized that there was something odd about this boy. Part of me said get away fast, but another part was curious and said stick around.

"Where do you live, young man?"

"Just over the hill in the castle. My father is prince of this territory, but he's off fighting the Turks, I think. He's gone a lot. Maybe, he'll be killed, then I can be the prince and be in charge. Someday..."

"That's no way to think of your father," I stated, although I didn't have particularly fond memories of my father, either, whoever he was.

"He's just a person I barely know. I think that I'm supposed to take over when he dies or something, but I don't know him at all. Sometimes I think he'd rather not have me around, but I'll show him. I've found a way to make myself invincible, immortal, then he won't be able to do anything to me."

"Careful what you wish for, kid. Being immortal may not be all that it's cracked up to be. Believe me, I know."

The lad eyed me up and down and then observed, "You're an odd sort, that's for sure. What are you, anyway?"

"The Minotaur, at your service. Perhaps you've heard of the legendary—no, not legendary—*mythological* half-human, half-bull beast, trapped in the Labyrinth, slain by the great Theseus of Athens?"

"No," the boy answered.

He was silent for a moment and then said, "Vlad."

"What?"

"Vlad, my name is Vlad. Vlad the third to be exact. Let's go back to the castle and I'll introduce you to dear Mother."

I gathered up the poor pooch in my arms and followed my new friend back to his big black, imposing castle.

"I'll also show you Ren. He's a little strange; has his own, bizarre ideas about life. Just humor him, he's really harmless."

I was starting to wonder what I was getting myself into, but curiosity got the best of me as we approached the huge castle and entered through its dark wooden doors. We stepped into an elaborate foyer, filled with tapestries, old weapons mounted on the wall, some rather bizarre sculptures, and half a dozen doors, leading, I presumed, to various chambers.

Vlad led me through the large middle door and we entered an even larger room, lighter and filled with elaborate cushioned furnishings and more tapestries and bizarre sculpture. When I say bizarre sculpture I don't mean abstract in the modern art sort of way. These carved figures were hideous chimeras, goats with human feet, huge chickens devouring people, a naked woman without a face and many others.

"Who is the artist?" I asked. "Who came up with the idea for such an unusual collection of sculptures?"

"That would be my mother," Vlad replied with a sigh.

At that moment I heard a loud, blood curdling shriek, and then Vlad gave a faint smile.

"That would be her now, she's finally awake. Mother keeps rather late hours and usually sleeps well into the afternoon. Sometimes, like today, she doesn't get up until well after sunset. It's best not to see her so soon after she gets up. Let's go to the North tower and find Rennie. I'll introduce you to Mother later."

We went through another huge door and then down a long dark corridor, up five flights of stairs until we stood outside a lone room at the top of the stairs, the top of the North tower, I assumed. Vlad took out a key and unlocked the door. He lit the candle that was just inside the door, illuminating the sparsely appointed room. There was a thin mat on the floor, a bucket, and some hay in one corner. On top of the hay I saw a boy, about the same age as Vlad, squatting and bouncing up and down. Every few minutes he reached into his pocket, pulled something out and popped it into his mouth. Then he would resume his bouncing.

"Ren, I've brought you a visitor," Vlad said in a soft and soothing voice. "He's not like any of the others. Come and see."

Ren turned his head and stared, then started his bouncing again, stopped and jumped to his feet.

"Well, you're an unusual looking soul," he observed, rattling off rapid fire words. "I'll bet you've seen lots of action. Are you a bull or a man or just bullish on men. Don't come too close to me; I don't want to be enchanted like you and turn into a bull or worse. When's your birthday? Mine was just last week, but I had to stay here in the tower. It's for my own good. But, it's OK, plenty of bugs coming through; yup, plenty of bugs to keep me young."

As he spoke a fly buzzed right in front of his face. In a flash his hand shot out and trapped the poor, unsuspecting insect. He shook his hand rapidly and popped the dazed bug in his mouth.

"Another tiny life added to my own," he observed.

Vlad must have noticed the look on my face as he started to explain.

"Renfield, here, is convinced that every live creature he consumes adds its life force to his own. Even though that fly is tiny, it has a life. He spends his days catching bugs and eating them. As you saw, he's very efficient. It saves a bit on the food bills, but is not the simplest path to immortality."

I thought for a moment and considered whether I should talk about my own experience with immortality, but decided it was best not to bring it up at this time. I wasn't really worried about being eaten alive, but it was also wise not to provide temptation.

"An interesting concept and not without a bit of validity, I suspect," I commented. "It will take years to know if his theory is correct. I can't say that consuming insects is my idea of fine dining, but at the same time, I've seen worse."

"It is an altogether disgusting habit, if you ask me," Vlad replied. "I think there are better ways to live forever. 'Life is in the blood,' I've heard it said. Drinking blood is the only sure way, at least that's my opinion."

"Disgustingness is in the eye of the beholder," I observed and then I decided to drop the whole topic and change the subject.

"Anything else of interest here in the castle?" I inquired.

Vlad's face lit up, "Of course, let's go out back and we can see the wolves."

Wolves? I thought. *Pets?* I felt a bit of trepidation, but I was still curious about this strange young man who seemed so sure of himself and had an intelligence that was rare and well beyond his years. We went to the rear of the castle into a courtyard and he let loose with a loud, shrill whistle.

In a few moments there was low growling from behind me and I turned to see a dozen grey wolves slowly approaching. I turned to my host but he was nowhere to be seen. I decided it was time to make a tactful retreat, but when I turned again to go back into the castle the way was blocked by the largest of the hungry looking beasts.

I shouldn't be so trusting went through my head as I looked around for some sort of weapon. Unfortunately, there was nothing but empty space as the wolves started creeping closer. I figured I was a goner as the vicious beasts moved in, now only a few feet away. I turned from one side to the other, doing my best to distract them and, foolishly, trying to make them think there were ten of me.

The big leader crouched, preparing to leap. He was licking his lips and was about to pounce when I heard another loud shrill whistle, slightly lower tone than the previous one. The wolves instantly stopped and lay down and I breathed a sigh of relief. Vlad walked out of the shadows, huge smile on his face and he started to laugh.

"For a huge fearsome beast, you sure looked scared. Just a bit of fun; come on, let's get back inside. I'm sure dinner is ready."

I followed him to the great dining hall, but I kept a lookout over my shoulder for any wayward "pets."

23.

I STAYED WITH VLAD FOR quite a while. The decrepit mongrel puppy grew into a robust mongrel dog, devoted to me, but always a bit wary of our unusual host. That first evening, I met Vlad's mother, a thin, pale woman of about thirty-five years with dark sunken eyes, and wild frizzy brown hair, who constantly wore long black dresses as if she were in perpetual mourning. She spoke very few words and those that she did utter came in short, staccato bursts.

"Thunder and lightning tonight," she would utter in her loud, shrill voice, and then be silent for several minutes. "Good weather for creation." And then more silence. "Creating art, I mean."

After this clarification she didn't talk for several days; she seemed to be spooked, although I really didn't think it was me. She hadn't even blinked at my appearance. I would often see her stealing quick glances at her son, but she would turn away just as quickly. I deduced that, in the absence of the father, the son was the true master of that castle, commanding his mother, Renfield, wolves, and only god knew what else. I also surmised that he was not a benevolent dictator.

To me, however, he offered nothing but deference. After the episode with the wolves he treated me as an honored guest. I had a luxurious bed chamber, food at any hour of the day or night, servants to attend to my every need, the now devoted dog, who I named Flavius, and my host's undivided attention.

It seems that young Vlad's curiosity was endless. He asked about the Labyrinth, about my many adventures, my philosophy on life and the world. He wondered aloud about the circumstances of my birth, the identity of my real father and, most of all, he asked me about my long life.

"You must have had a god for a father," he stated one day. "Think about it. How could you live these thousands of years if a mere mortal, or even that fine bull, had been your father? No, it must have been an immortal deity that sired you and now you have some sort of immortality force running through your body. I wish I could be like you, never worry about dying, alive forever."

"Be careful what you wish for, young Vlad," I replied. "It's true I've lived a long time and I just keep on living. But, there have been a lot of years of complete boredom. Wasted years trapped within the Labyrinth. A very high price to pay, if you ask me, and such loneliness. I think that's the worst thing of all. Maybe it's my own doing, but I think the gods have played a great trick on me. Set me free from the solitude of the Labyrinth at times, free to mingle with other beings, men and cows, only to fill my life with malice and disappointment and to make me yearn for the safety of the Labyrinth's walls and the peace that I feel when I'm inside."

Vlad didn't respond at all to my words of wisdom. He was silent for a while and looked disappointed. After a few minutes he spoke.

"It doesn't have to be that way," he said softly. "Maybe for you the long years have kept you isolated. Maybe it's all your choice. I don't know why I think so much about death. At times I worry about what happens afterwards. Is there an afterlife? Are we just gone, becoming dust and forgotten after a month of superficial mourning? I just don't think I can deal with such an unknown."

It was one of the few reflective moments I ever saw him have. Most of the time he was in charge: resolute, confident, and determined. And even though he worried about his own life, he had absolutely no regard for anyone else. I say this because of the way he treated everyone that surrounded him. His mother was kept locked away most of the time, either in her room or her studio. She joined us for dinner frequently, but I never saw her outside the confines of the castle and never outdoors. Renfield was confined to his tower. Vlad often would disappear for hours at a time after which I would see him coming from the direction of the tower. I don't know if he was Renfield's benefactor or tormentor. I suspect it was both.

As for me, I had free reign of the castle and the grounds, except for Mother's room and studio. Books were unheard of at that time, at least in Vlad's castle, not even a Bible. I spent the time recording my thoughts in Latin, a language foreign to that household. I wrote about all my trials and tribulations, a record of all that had happened. I was aware of the mythology surrounding my name and wanted to have something at hand to set the record straight.

I had been at it for about two months when I started to notice some of the unusual occurrences that transpired in that gloomy castle. Mother, I noticed, waxed and waned between slightly pale and death warmed over. Vlad was almost manic at times, such episodes always coinciding with his mother's worst moments. The art work became more and more morbid and there seemed to be an obsession with death. It all became a bit too bizarre for me and I decided it was time to leave. It was common for no one to be about at midday and so I grabbed my few possessions and walked out the front door. As I approached the castle gate I was suddenly surrounded by a litany of growls.

Barring my way were Vlad's "pets." I quickly deduced that I was somewhat more than a guest and returned to the castle. That night at dinner Vlad uttered a few words.

"The wolves were out and about a bit earlier than usual today. I suspect there was an unwelcome visitor snooping about. The pack scared him away. I trust that there will be no unwelcome guests for a while. I'm sure, Minotaur, you realize that I am very selective in who I allow to visit. Privacy is very important for Mother, for Renfield, for you and for me. Don't you agree?"

I thought for a while before I answered. I was growing uneasy in that place. There was an eerie gloom and I sensed that I was doomed to end up like Mother or Renfield if I remained too long. Although I couldn't quite pin it all down, I was sure that something akin to the tower, or worse, was in my future. It wasn't long before it all came to pass, something I should have anticipated had I been paying attention to my hosts words instead of thinking about wolves and insects and bizarre, morbid artwork.

It was actually only a few days later that it happened. I suppose my feeble attempt to escape pushed my host to act. I was sleeping in my chambers after a large and unusually sumptuous meal. I retired earlier than usual, perhaps I had been drugged, perhaps it was the food or wine. Whatever the reason, I was in a deep sleep when I had an unusual dream. I dreamt I was being chased by a giant snake. Although I should have been able to outrun such a beast, the snake was catching up to me. It finally caught me and wrapped itself around my body, holding my arms tight against my side. First it stared into my eyes, its gaze beautiful and mesmerizing. Then, with a quick dart of its head, it plunged its fangs into my neck. Blood squirted out and, at that moment, I awoke to see the real snake.

I had been bound with some very stout rope. There was a long, deep gash in my neck and blood was spurting out, being gathered up in a large receptacle being held by Renfield. Vlad, the real snake, was sitting opposite me, a rather serious look on his face.

"You're special, unique," he said softly. "Truly immortal, filled with a life force that never diminishes. Truly, the life is in the blood and now your life will be mine. The blood of others provided nothing. One may live a normal life by drinking it, but to live forever—that is in your blood. A gift from the gods? Or a curse. Whichever it is, I'll possess it and you will be released from your solitude. You shall have the freedom that death brings."

I was becoming lightheaded as the stream of blood slowed to a trickle and then I blacked out completely, my last thought was that I would return to the Labyrinth forever.

It was, however, not to be. I have no doubt that I knocked on Death's door. Fortunately, Death was out getting a new shroud or something. Vlad, coveting his prize, left me in a crumpled heap on the hard, stone castle floor, assuming that my life had drained away with my blood. Of course I was left weakened and in shock, but I was very much alive. Oddly enough it was the wolves that saved me. For whatever reason they decided to adopt me as one of their own. They formed a circle around me, laid against me keeping me warm and, over a few days time I recovered. I was able to crawl to the fountain outside and drink some water which filled me with new strength. The wolves brought food, and I suppose my will to live was stronger than the call to return to the Labyrinth.

I wasn't sure exactly what else happened, but after I ate something I passed out again. This time I awoke in my bed with Vlad staring down at me.

"I will keep you and your blood with me. We shall live forever, you and I. Now that I have your blood and life within my veins I will never die."

Being a perpetual soda fountain for a crazy teenager was not how I wanted to spend my years. Unfortunately, Vlad had different plans. I was shackled to the bed, and now I was sure that my room was a prison. In all the thousands of years I had lived, I had never felt so hopeless.

I regained my strength over the next few weeks and was able to get up, walk, and eat. I felt completely normal in every way. I started to plot my escape which was no simple task. I was in a room with two windows crisscrossed with heavy iron bars. The walls were solid stone and the only door was made of heavy wood and bolted from the outside. The windows looked out over the courtyard, a sheer drop of about one hundred feet. And, I was chained to the wall, my shackles long enough to allow me to walk to the window and peer through my prison bars, but that was it. The dog was nowhere to be found, finally, I suspected, victim to Vlad's unsocial demeanor. *Probably better off*, I thought.

One day, while I was pacing back and forth, trying for the thousandth time to loosen the bonds that held me, Vlad paid me the compliment of a visit. He was looking more robust than usual and even a bit more youthful, with his smooth white skin and eyes that twinkled with a striking blue light. He held up a glass jar half-filled with a reddish-brown powdery substance.

"Your blood," he explained. "This is your blood, dried up, but still potent. As you can see, it agrees with me and as long as I possess you, I will remain the youthful lad you see now. But now that you've recovered I will need to replenish my supply."

There was a loud grinding noise and I felt my chains tighten. A winch in the ceiling gradually shortened my shackles and I soon found myself hanging upside down and completely helpless. Vlad produced a long sharp blade.

"Don't squirm," he advised. It will take longer and I may lose some your precious blood."

Despite his warning, I still fought, but all for naught. With a single, sharp, skillful thrust and slice the razor found its mark and, once again, my blood shot forth, caught in the bucket Renfield was holding. I guess I didn't hold perfectly still and some of it dotted the walls and floor. I don't know if it was the loss of blood or the sight of Vlad, licking my blood off the walls and floor, but I was overcome by a wave of nausea, vomited all over Renfield, and then I passed out.

This time I awoke in my bed, the new neck wound freshly dressed, a pitcher of water on the nightstand. *Need to guard one's meal ticket*, I thought. An endless lifetime serving as the fountain of youth to a sociopathic teenager was not how I intended to spend my days. As I lay in bed recovering from this latest insult, I studied my prison ever so closely.

The chains were bolted to the stone wall opposite the barred window. They went from the wall to the winches in the ceiling and then to me. As I stated before, my fetters gave me enough freedom to look out the window and walk about the room, but that was the limit.

The bars on the window appeared worn. Even so, I had tested them previously and found that they were pretty solid, unlikely to be easily broken. It seemed hopeless.

I recovered more quickly this time, although I kept my return to health a secret. I was able to get up unobserved and had opportunity to examine the bars on the windows more closely. They were pounded into the stone and I surmised that they probably only went in far enough to hold them in place. Powerful drills were not available; the stone would have been chiseled away and then mortar used to fill in any gaps. The mortar would be the weak point and this is the point I started my attack.

I twisted my head and used the point of my horn to scrape along the top of the bar. A small bit of mortar fell to the floor. I tried the same on the bottom and was able to loosen a bit more. It actually didn't take very long until I was able to wiggle the bars back and forth. Whenever I heard footsteps approaching I packed the loose mortar around the bars and jumped back into bed. After a few days I was able to remove the bars completely. Luckily, the window seemed to be just big enough for me to crawl out. Step one was done.

Next came loosening the chains; not from the wall, rather from the winches. I could look through the wooden boards in the ceiling and see the crank and the wheel and how they were fixed to the wooden planks. With a bit of manipulation of the chains I'd be able to free them and give myself more slack to move about over a wider area.

Finally, the bolts holding the chains to the wall were examined and this is where I thought I'd be stymied. The bolts were at least an inch across and probably embedded in solid stone. Even with my great weight at the end they hadn't shown the slightest sign of weakening. Chipping away at the stone would take a thousand years. I looked for alternatives, but there wasn't any obvious solution. But then again, maybe there was, the proverbial weakest link. Each chain must have a weak point and, under the proper stress, this weak point would give out, I hoped. It was already deep into the night when I finished my preparations. Tomorrow I decided to put all my theories to the test and, I hoped, make my escape.

24.

I DIDN'T SLEEP A WINK that night. I spent the remaining hours of darkness playing various scenarios over and over in my head. Clean escape; escape but with complications; utter failure; chickening out. In the end I decided nothing really mattered—success failure, life, death, what difference did it make? I'd lived for thousands of years, experienced far more misery than joy and, although my current situation was the most wretched of all, failure would only be a minor set-back. Vlad wouldn't put an end to me; after all, who would knowingly destroy the Fountain of Youth?

As soon as the sun's rays started creeping through my window, I was up. I began shaking my chains and was able to jostle them off the winches in about an hour. I found that this afforded me an extra fifteen feet or so of length. I pulled the bars out of the window and stepped back, looking at every-thing, checking the chains and overall psyching myself up for the ride that was to come.

I stood by the door to my room and then raced towards the open window and dove out. I launched a beautiful swan dive into the open air. As planned, I shot out and then back towards the window below mine, hoping to smash through, while also hoping that my chains would snap and I'd be free to make a mad dash through the castle, out the front door and on my way to the next disaster.

Reality set in, however, as I smashed into the window and didn't break through. Two of my chains snapped, but two remained intact. I began to kick against the window as shouts came from my room. Vlad, Mother, and Renfield were looking down at me and yelling. The wolves circled below and there I was, dangling fifty feet above the ground, held fast by the chains around my right wrist and left ankle.

Slowly, I felt myself being pulled up, back to my prison. Then there was a sudden jerk and I fell another ten feet, now being held only by my right wrist. I have to say it was not the most comfortable position I'd ever been in. Once again I started ascending, ever so slowly. I guess I was pretty heavy. I'd move a few inches and then stop; move a few more inches and then stop again. I passed the window below my room and continued rising. It seemed like hours and the pain in my wrist was excruciating, as I continued to inch towards my prison cell. A hand grabbed one of my horns and started to pull on it. Then, just as I'd reached a level where I could see the triumphant smirk on Vlad's youthful face, I kicked against the wall and caused them to lose their grip. I plummeted down to below the windows, stopped for a moment, and then fell a bit farther. I looked up to see arms vainly trying to hold the chain. It was their attempts to retrieve me that actually afforded me a fairly gentle descent. Once my foot hit the ground I gave a sharp tug on the chain which flew out the window and settled on the ground at my feet. The wolves quietly sniffed me and the chain and then withdrew. I sauntered out the front gate to freedom. I thought I'd seen the end of Vlad, and I had, at least for quite a long time.

I made my way west, away from Transylvania, over rivers, through thick forests, over low hills and higher mountains. In general, I avoided people as much as possible and I really wasn't sure where I should go. I was getting the sense that the world was passing me by, that a beast like myself had no place in the modern world of the fifteenth century. I'm not sure how long I wandered about, but I eventually came upon a monastery. It was late at night and I remember I was tired after the day's walking.

I simply knocked on the gate and was greeted by a hooded monk. He didn't carry any torch or lantern, the only light came from the faint moon. He opened the door for me and I followed him inside. He had no problem finding his way in the dark and he led me up some stairs to a stark room. Inside was a window that was open to the night air, a straw mat on the stone floor, a thin blanket, a pail filled with water and another empty bucket. He held the door for me and left me after I entered, all the time never uttering a single sound. I assumed I was welcome to stay. I lay down on the mat and quickly fell asleep. The warm sun shining through the window woke me. Nothing had changed, except there was a monk's robe neatly folded at the foot of my "bed," which I put on. I had trouble fitting it over my horns, but was able to poke them through the hood. *I'm a monk, now,* I believed. I wasn't sure what that would entail. I soon learned that being a monk, at least in the beginning, meant more solitude.

Monastic life required a great deal of silence, of solitary sequestration, of prayer and devotion to God. I was pretty good at the first two and faked the rest. I stayed in that room day after day, locked away, without food, only the pail of water which they changed daily. I learned later that they decided I was either a great sinner, deep into repentance, or the most pious of all beings, embarking on such a prolonged fast. They were wrong on both accounts. I was truly disgusted with humanity, be they monks or psychopathic monsters. I needed time to myself, alone, back in a self-imposed Labyrinth. That stark room at the monastery was just the right place at the right time.

I spent day after day in that room thinking about everything that had happened to me over the thousands of years I had lived. I relived adventure in the jungle, triumphs and failures, reflected on my unusual birth, wondered who my true father was, tried to logically deduce where my proper place in society was. Was I a cow or a man? Should I seek residence among the livestock of the land, try my hand as a bull? Maybe I was really of the aristocracy, born to be King of some fantastic and, probably faraway land. Was there only one God or many gods, and if such a being as God really existed did I find favor in his eyes?

I reflected on my experience in the cave, the dead Jesus rising up and filling that cave with such light that I still marveled over it more than a thousand years later. I assumed that He really hadn't been dead and that it was all some sort of elaborate trick. But then I'd feel that spot on my head where He touched me so long ago and a feeling of warmth would fill me. I wasn't sure why. And there were the dreams I'd experienced, dreams that seemed so real, that took me back in time, that made me feel like I had been in each place. Dreams that carried messages that I did not understand.

I think it was almost a month before any of those monks built up the courage or cared enough to actually enter my little room. It was Brother Dominick who came, the youngest and least experienced of all of them. I'm sure the more senior monks considered him the most expendable, that is, if I was actually Satan or some other demon.

He lightly tapped on my door, I suspect fully anticipating that he would be turned away, but I answered with a bit of a gruff. "Hello, come in." The door slowly creaked open and a slight, wisp of a monk sheepishly entered. He pulled his hood down as he entered and I stood to greet him.

"Minotaur," I said a bit gruffly and I stuck out my right hand, which he took weakly. I grasped his hand tightly and gave it a good shake.

"Glad to meet you, Brother..."

"Dominick," he answered. "I'm Brother Dominick. I represent the monks that reside here. The others have charged me with asking some questions. You don't mind, do you? Because if this is a bad time I could come back later."

"Now or later, it doesn't matter to me. The one thing I seem to have an unlimited supply of is time. But you're here, so we might as well chat. So, tell me, Brother Dominick, how long have you been a monk? How many of you live here? What type of monks are you? Any women here?"

My timid guest seemed a bit overwhelmed, so I tried to put him at ease.

"Can I offer you some water? I'm sorry, but room service did not bring me a glass," I offered, trying to mind my manners and not send him screaming back to his elders.

"Er... Nothing for me, thanks. Do you mind if I sit?"

"Not at all. The floor is yours."

He sat down in the corner as far away from me as possible and closed his eyes.

"We're Augustinian monks," he began, "dedicated to following the path laid out by St. Augustine a thousand years ago. There are about one hundred twenty of us, all men. We spend our days in prayer and meditation, reading and copying sacred Scripture, and doing all the work that's necessary to keep Jesus' words and this place going."

"Why did you become a monk?" I queried.

"I didn't have much choice. I was heading down a path of sure destruction. It was either join the monastery or forfeit my life. I'd rather not talk about me; tell me about yourself, the fearsome 'Minotaur' of myth and legend."

"I suppose my presence would raise a few questions," I answered.

So, I told him my story. He sat there, apparently fascinated, barely moving for the entire day, as I rambled on about all I'd seen and done. When I finished, he stood up and breathed a sigh.

"Amazing," was all he said. The evening bell rang and he looked out the window. "Have to run, evening prayer calls.

I'll come to see you tomorrow. You are welcome to come to prayer."

"No, thank you," I answered. "I tried praying once and it was not a pretty sight. I do look forward to having another little talk."

I shook his hand and he left, off to report to his superiors no doubt.

I expected visits from some of the other monks, but only Brother Dominick came. It made me wonder what he had told the others, but I really didn't mind. Dominick came just after lunch each day, bringing me the days repast, usually some bread and thin soup. Food never mattered much to me. My companion always looked longingly at my bit of food and most days I shared it with him or gave the whole of it to him. He usually devoured it ravenously. Perhaps that was one of the reasons he had discouraged the others from visiting. It didn't matter; I was glad that I could be of some benefit to him.

He had been sent to the monastery at age fifteen. Apparently he had been in a great deal of trouble, something about a girl and a baby. I'll spare you the sordid details, but I could tell he missed them both. The romantic in me decided that this family simply had to be reunited. Of course, being the Minotaur and living in an isolated monastery posed a bit of a problem. At first I thought Dominick only needed a bit of encouragement, enough courage to defy those who'd put him here, but I soon realized that it was going to take something more.

The monastery sometimes seemed almost like a prison. As best as I could tell, there was only one way in or out and all the windows had iron bars. One of the more senior monks was always in attendance at the entrance and only senior monks were allowed to leave. Dominick, being the most junior and also a bit suspect was never allowed near the door. His job was washing: floors, robes, dishes, pots, and everything else. Still, he found the time to visit almost every day. He loved to hear stories of days long past. He gradually opened up to me.

He really had wanted to be an artist, paint portraits and such. His father was a vintner; his mother tended the house and cared for his two brothers and three sisters. He was the oldest. He showed me some of his artwork, beautiful sketches of the other monks, some of the animals around the monastery, scenes of forests and streams, all beautifully conceived. After a few weeks of visits I told him I'd find some way for him to escape.

That day, after he'd left, but while the sun was still out, I studied the area outside my window. All I could see were stone walls and the forest about a hundred yards away. I remembered that the road was nothing more than a dirt trail, rocky and meandering, the monastery sitting at the bottom of a hill. The village was about five miles away, up the hill and at the end of a lake. Dominick said his lost love could be found at the Wild Horse Inn. Her father apparently was the owner. He also told me that she would be entering a convent when she was sixteen, which was only six weeks away. I needed a plan and I needed it fast.

25.

THAT NIGHT I LAY ON my thin straw mattress pondering different possibilities when providence dropped the answer in my lap. I heard some voices outside my window and also the whinnying of a horse. I had only heard the chirping of crickets or the occasional howl of a timber wolf prior to this. I looked out the window and saw one of the monks riding away towards the woods, his robe flowing in the wind and his hood pulled down around his shoulders, illuminated by a bright full moon. Then I heard the creaking sound of a heavy door closing and was able to catch of a glimpse of a stone door in the wall adjacent to my window.

Horses... a secret doorway; just what were these monks up to? I stayed awake the rest of the night, assuming that the AWOL monk would return before daybreak. Sure enough, just before dawn and morning prayer, I heard the sound of cantering hoof beats and I saw him return, his hood up, although he seemed a bit unsteady on his mount. I heard him singing softly to himself a bawdy song that was popular at that time, particularly among the degenerate theater crowd.

He's been to one of those travelling minstrel shows, no doubt, I thought. I'd heard of such shows, full of debauchery, performed by the lowest of lowlifes. *So much for renouncing worldly deeds and material.* I suddenly felt much better about plotting to help Brother Dominick and I actually decided that he'd be much better off away from what I was beginning to believe was a palace of hypocrisy, the worst of all sins, as far as I was concerned.

The next night I donned the robe the monks had provided and ventured out of my little room. The monastery was a maze of hallways and it seemed the monks didn't believe in torches to illuminate the passages. I stumbled about until I found the stairs, almost falling to my death as I missed the first step, lost my balance, and rolled down the curved staircase, smashing my head on the stone landing. It took me few minutes to gather my bearings, but I finally figured out the way to the secret door. It turned out that there were horses stabled just inside the door. I was surprised that Brother Dominick was unaware of this "back door." Making an escape would be child's play. A little diversion and he'd be off to freedom and his waiting family.

The next day I told him my plan. His face lit up with a big smile and he shook my hand, then he pranced around the room with joy and then shook my hand again. I told him he had to be ready to go at a moment's notice. The signal to leave would be unmistakable.

I didn't plan anything very elaborate; after all it was only the fifteenth century. I would start a fire at the opposite end of the monastery, big enough to draw all the other monks' attention, but not so big that it would burn the place down. I decided that the next day at dusk would be best. It was at this moment that I realized that starting a big fire, secretly, without drawing suspicion to myself would not be as simple as I thought. What to burn, how to get the blaze started, how to keep it properly contained all were important considerations and all were made a bit more difficult by the fact that there were no torches or open fires at that monastery, the monks living an ascetic life. The only fire was in the kitchen and sneaking in there and stealing fire would be quite a trick. I was beginning to understand how Prometheus must have felt.

After all these considerations I hit on a different scheme, one that was bit more dangerous for me, but safer for everyone else: Mad Cow. Most of the monks knew nothing about me and only two of them had even seen me: the one on duty the night I arrived and Dominick. A bit of a ruckus at the main gate would be more than enough to draw everyone's attention and allow Brother Dominick to waltz away to freedom and his waiting family. I realized I would be taking a bit of a risk; it was probable that monks would be frightened by my display and decide to put me out, but I figured it was worth it. After all this was for family and amore and what could be more important than that. A bit of inconvenience for me was a small price to pay to reunite this man with his sweetheart and daughter.

The next evening, precisely as the sun was settling down in the west, I started my show. I began with a loud roar and then battered the front gate with a heavy log and then some more roaring. I managed to froth up my mouth and, as the crowd of monks started to gather, I rammed the wooden gate with my horns, not once, not twice, I rammed that gate twenty six times, until I'd almost knocked myself silly. I went on with my show for nearly thirty minutes and I was sure that all the monks were there. I hoped that Brother Dominick had made his escape as I had developed a rip roaring headache and didn't think I could go on for more than a few minutes more. It was at this point that the monks surprised me. It began with a thin, withered old monk, one of the leaders no doubt.

As I carried on, he knelt down to the ground and started to pray. At first I couldn't understand what he was saying, he was chanting softly. Gradually the other monks joined him on the ground and his prayers became louder. I heard him pray for forgiveness for me, for my soul, for my release from Satan. They thought I was possessed by the Devil; perhaps I was. As their prayers grew to a dull roar I stopped my antics. I had grown tired and I was sure Dominick had been given enough time to escape. I turned and started to walk away. The same elderly monk came up from behind and hugged me and said:

"The evil one has been driven away. You will be made whole. Have faith in God."

He took me by the hand and led me back to my little room and left me alone. As a matter of fact, they all left me alone, for a long time. They did bring me a Bible and some other Scripture to read; later on I procured many of the Greek and Roman classics: Homer, Aristophanes, Virgil, and other similar works. But none of those monks came to visit. I stayed in that room for years, alone, reading, pondering the human and bovine condition. I suppose it was the taint of the devil that kept them away, but, over all those years as I thought about it all, it occurred to me: Aren't we all tainted by the Devil?

I'm not sure if I stayed there by choice or by some Divine intervention, but I stayed, back in the Labyrinth. I completely lost track of time and the monks left me alone, only bringing food and water and other basic necessities.

Finally, after decades of solitude, Brother Martin came.

Brother Martin, now there was a fine, intelligent monk, a little confused at first, but a man who taught me a great deal. I think he was in his late twenties when he came to visit. He was curious about the ancient hermit who had never so much as put his toe out of his room for so many years. Looking back I'm not sure why I kept my self locked away for so long. Perhaps it was stubbornness, perhaps it was my long held out hope that someone would come to me. I do know that, with nothing better to do, I read and reread the Scriptures hundreds of times. I was quite the Bible scholar, despite my unbelief.

Getting back to Brother Martin, he had also studied the Scriptures and was considered a very learned professor. I'm not sure how long he'd been at the monastery when I heard his knock on my door. I remember feeling a bit of excitement at that moment, quite a natural feeling considering I'd been in complete solitude for so long.

"Come in," I answered in a quiet voice.

A monk entered, his face shielded by the hood of his robe. As soon as he entered and took a look around, he stopped. I heard a loud "gasp" and then he took two steps back. I was sure he was going to make a hasty exit, but instead he sighed, took a deep breath, and entered the room.

"Hello..." he whispered as he closed the door behind him.

"Minotaur... call me Minotaur. Perhaps you've read about me. I hear that I'm well represented in ancient Greek myth," I said, offering him a spot on the floor. He quickly crossed himself and pulled a wooden cross from his robe, prominently displaying it, no doubt warding off evil spirits.

"According to myth you were killed," he reported.

"That's why it's myth and not historical fact," I replied.

"According to monastery legend you were demon-possessed and Old Brother Andrew cast the demon out."

"Brother Andrew certainly believed that, but really I was helping another Brother escape."

"Oh yes, I've heard of Brother Dominick and how he escaped during all the excitement. He died a short time later."

My heart sank at this news.

"Really, what happened?"

"It seems he went from here to the nearest brothel. He stole some fine icons from the sanctuary and used them to pay for his brief prodigal life. Unfortunately, after he'd used up all his resources he took up with a married woman whose husband was away. The husband returned unexpectedly and found the two of them in a rather embarrassing position. Let's just say that Brother Dominick tried to get away by jumping out the window only he forgot that he was on the third floor. That was the end of him."

His story left me a bit perplexed. What happened to his young wife and baby? Brother Martin filled me in.

"Brother Dominick's tale is told to every new member of our monastery. It seems he was sent here because of some trouble with a young girl, the thirteen-year-old daughter of the town's mayor. And there was the stealing and constant lying. He was considered a hopeless case and he was intended for prison. His parents had some influence, however, and they managed to secure him a place here. Well, I've told you the rest."

He saw me shake my head as my faith in the depravity of humans was reinforced once again.

"It seems that complete humans like you are all the same," I stated. "You never fail to live down to the lowest levels. I've met very few men and women over the years that would be considered truly righteous. As a matter of fact, there's only one man that I've met that didn't have any apparent flaws and it was really only for a brief moment, except in a dream."

After this statement, Brother Martin sat in silence for several minutes.

"You know, Brother Minotaur," he finally spoke, "what you've just said is very interesting. It may be the key to everything that's been gnawing at me since I became a monk and the reason the Devil can never completely triumph. Thanks."

He seemed to enter a fog as he absentmindedly got up from the floor and left my room. I truly liked him, although I could sense that he was troubled, that he was working through some sort of personal crisis. I hoped he would come back and I hoped that I could help him find a sense of peace.

He did come back over and over, almost every day. He would always talk about the Church; something was wrong with the whole of the Church; something was missing; this was what he was struggling with. The Church asked for so much: confession of all one's sins, obedience to the sacraments, and so much more.

"I try and try," he said. "My confession runs four or five hours and I still forget some sins. I'm supposed to give the mass soon, but how can any man administer the communion sacrament unless he is without sin? The bread is the body of our Lord. Only He is perfect, only He can say, 'This is my body; this is my blood.' "

I thought about what he said for a long time and then I answered, "I've seen your Lord in person. I was in the cave with him. I saw him laid to rest, shrouded, dead. But the darkness vanished and was replaced by bright light. He pushed the stone away as if it was a feather and he touched me, right here."

I pointed to my head.

"Since that moment this spot has always been a place of comfort for me and I really don't know why. I don't believe in any one god, but this Jesus, this man you call 'Christ,' I do know that he was special above all men."

It was Brother Martin's turn to be silent. A huge smile filled his face and he excitedly jumped up and started to pace rapidly back and forth.

"That's it, that's what the Church has forgotten. Jesus died for us, took our sins upon Himself. He has done all the work. It's what the Apostle Paul said over and over and over. Christ died for us and anyone who believes that one single fact and accepts it as the truth, then their faith grants them Christ's righteousness and His perfect life becomes theirs. That is the true Gospel and all the works and indulgences mean nothing and are nothing."

His joy and excitement were contagious as we both started jumping up and down. Finally he stopped.

"We've got to share this with the other monks, with the Church, with the world. I'll need your help. I'll be back tomorrow and we'll go to work, writing this down for all humanity."

The next day he came loaded down with paper and pen and ink. He started writing his thoughts, his interpretations, his views of the Scripture, the Church, Jesus, the Gospel and his objections. He knew the Bible pretty well, but at times certain passages slipped his mind and he would ask me. I'd read that whole book hundreds of times over the years and, although I was never a believer, I could recite large parts from memory and certainly knew where certain sayings could be found.

He started to develop his theses, writing each down and numbering them. Statements of fact clearly delineated in Scripture, areas where the Church had gone astray and how it could return to the true Gospel as stated over and over again by Jesus and his apostles.

"This will return the Church to its spiritual roots," he stated with a joy and infectious enthusiasm. "The Gospel is for all men to hear, to study, and to embrace. These 140 theses have to be heard all the way to Rome. We'll post them on the notice board tomorrow: All Hallow's Eve."

He left his writings with me and I promised to bring them early the next morning. I looked them over and was impressed with his interpretation of the words I'd read over and over again. Reading done not as a way to teach myself or improve myself, rather strictly out of boredom and lack of anything else to entertain me. And although I'd memorized so much of it, I thought that it was not for me. I wasn't fully man and "the Gospel," as Brother Martin called it, was not for a half-breed mutant. However, I kept my promise and brought his 140 "theses" early the next morning.

He met me with a hammer and tacks and he nailed the first page to the wall and then the second. He was preparing to hammer the third when a strong wind came up just as I was handing the page to him. The last 45 theses blew away with that gale as we ran after it. However, it just seemed to rise higher and higher, and eventually we lost it in the bright morning sun. I don't know where it ended up, probably some-where in France.

We went back to the bulletin board and decided we'd have to settle for ninety-five theses. Despite the loss, Brother Martin seemed pleased and he was sure the other monks would be overjoyed at his new discovery and eventually the Pope himself would read those words and return the Church to the state that had been intended by Jesus, Paul, and Peter.

"I feel at peace for the first time in my life," he told me. "I no longer feel Satan's presence. The truth of the Gospel has set me free and it must be made so for all the people. The words of Scripture need to be made accessible to everyone, not just monks and priests and scholars. The shoemaker, the baker, the lowliest servant, the Gospel is for everyone."

Of course, you must be aware of what really happened. Martin Luther was cast out of the Church, the Pope was definitely not pleased, and a revolution began, a revolution of thought, which is never a bad thing.

I must add that Brother Martin was a good man in many ways, and having read the Bible over and over, I agree with most of his ideas, but he also had a few flaws. He only wanted to hear his own argument and pretty much closed his mind to interpretations that differed from his own. I for one can't say I ever could discern truth and from fantasy. Look at me; am I a living myth or just a mutant living a life of misery? A life trapped between two worlds, not belonging to either? I couldn't stay at the monastery after Brother Martin's revolt. The uproar and controversy threatened to engulf me, so, I left.

26.

I WANDERED AWAY FROM GERMANY into Switzerland. For a while I lived among the cows, but I found I'd lost my enthusiasm for the bovine life. Also, it seemed that the Swiss farmers were far more attentive to their charges than shepherds in other herds I had encountered previously. They drove me away time after time. I feared that the bullish part of my life had come to an end. But I had also soured on humanity, again. The bickering and pointless argument and frequent violence of men was hard for me to stomach. I left Switzerland and headed for the most isolated desolate place on the planet: The Himalayan Mountains.

I set my sights on a cave, any cave, thousands of miles away from humanity and thousands of feet above any soul, human or bovine. I didn't care about food or water or anything. I'd sunk into the lowest funk of my long life and all I wanted was solitude. I found a tall mountain and managed to climb up to a level where, when I looked down, all I'd see were ant-like people in a tiny village thousands of feet below. I didn't start any fire, brought only a small amount of food, ate snow, and sat and reflected, thankful for the quiet seclusion and complete lack of meddlesome, irritating, self-centered, vicious humans.

I stayed in my cave for years and years, alone, anonymous, and perfectly content. Of course, mostly what I did was think. I thought about everything I'd seen over the years and, in my head, I recorded it all. My written record had been lost, but the memories—the good, the bad, the ugly, and the sublime—remained. *It'll make a great book someday*, I thought.

But all good things come to an end and so it had to be with this sojourn back into the Labyrinth. To this day I have no idea how it happened, how knowledge of my existence leaked out or how or why I was elected wise old sage. All I know is that people started scaling that precipice to stand outside my cave and ask me questions. I remember the first time like it was yesterday.

"Oh, great wise one, tell me the way to true happiness."

Can you believe it? Me, a great wise sage? I was taken aback, and wasn't exactly sure how to answer. I told him to wait as I pondered his question. He was very patient, because I kept him waiting for two days. I kept hoping that my procrastinating would discourage him, but no such luck. Finally, I felt obliged to give an answer.

"The birds fly free and mate in the spring, while fish swim in open waters."

It was just nonsense, but that fellow listened intently, sat with a serious look on his face for at least three hours, then gave a big smile and left. I still don't know what he thought it all meant, but I certainly made some sort of impact. A few days later another person showed up.

"Oh, wise and powerful one, how can I find true love?"

What was wrong with these people? I didn't say anything until the next day, but, once again, that person just sat outside in the frigid mountain air, not moving, fearful of missing my great counsel. I was stuck again. *Something even more outrageous is in order*, I decided.

"Clouds cannot be held, but the rain falls to the ground."

That'll discourage them from bothering me anymore.

But, no such luck. They kept coming and coming. At first it was every few days or once a week. Then it was everyday, then two or three a day. No peace, it was driving me crazy.

Every time I'd settle down, ready to sit and think, or try to get up to go to the bathroom, a voice would sound, usually meek at first, but then, if I didn't answer right away, it would grow more belligerent and demanding as if I *owed* the requesting party a response. Luckily, not one of these sorry interlopers had the nerve to actually come inside the cave. Rumors abounded that I was some sort of monster. It seems none of these seekers realized the irony, they were searching for answers, but the source of this knowledge would just as well devour them as help them. I suppose this element of fear lent some form of legitimacy to their endeavors. It was becoming annoying, however. Still, they came.

"Should I have children?"
Little sprouts are easily trampled, leaving barren soil.

"How can I be rich?"
Idleness is the gift of the flocks; remember that water flows downhill.

And, always my favorite:

"Oh great wise one, what is the meaning of life?"
Life is a bountiful ocean, filled with dung.

Or

Life is a dead cow, worthless, but it can still make you sick.

Or

Life is just one thing.

That last one always brought a smile to my face, while the questioner was duly impressed with how deep and profound it was.

This nonsense went on for years, but one incident forced me to put a stop to it.

It was at night (isn't it always?) when she came, which was a bit unusual. The treachery of the mountain, fear of the unknown, the comfort of the daylight, whatever the reason, no one had ever come to me at night before this. Perhaps she was embarrassed to show her face during the day or perhaps it had taken her all the daytime hours to build up the courage to approach, I really don't know and never had the opportunity to find out. Her voice was soft and sweetly melodic, but also filled with despair and tragedy.

"Great one, I need your counsel. I feel so terribly unworthy to approach one such as you, but I can only place my hope in your great knowledge and wisdom," she spoke, so softly, barely audible.

Her voice touched me in a way that none of the others had. I moved closer to the door where I could see her silhouette in the bright moonlight which illuminated the night. She was of slight build and her hair was long, reaching well below her shoulders. She wore fine jewelry which sparkled in the moonlight. Truly she was a fine woman, yet even her dimly lit figure spoke of a life of hopelessness.

She continued, her voice slightly louder, "I am afraid and I don't know who to turn to. My life is a waking nightmare, filled with pain and suffering."

Her voice wavered and then she went silent for a while. She let out a great sigh and I sensed she was going to leave.

"What troubles you, my dear?" I asked as gently as I could.

"My child," she said and then burst into tears. "My child's life is threatened by a great and terrible danger," she cried between sobs. "My life will soon end and then my Mata will become the villainous fiend's next victim. Tell me what I can do?" And she broke down into uncontrollably wails of cries and tears.

"What is this great danger you are facing, sweet girl?" I asked, expecting it to be some trivial and unsubstantiated threat, a mythical wild beast or demons that didn't exist.

I suspect she hadn't anticipated such a direct question; my reputation for being obscure and cryptic had spread throughout the land.

"My husband," she whispered. "It's my husband. He beats me almost every day and now that my son is growing up, he will start beating him soon."

It was my turn to let out a short gasp. A flippant, absurd answer would not do.

"Such a man is the greatest of cowards and villains. You must escape with your son," I answered.

"Great one, I cannot escape. My husband is very powerful with many allies among the leaders in our village. If I should try to leave and fail, my life would be even worse."

I was beginning to see that this was no simple problem. She waited patiently outside the cave while I sat in silence trying to come up with a solution. Finally, I decided that I was the only solution; I would personally deliver her and her son.

"Return home, my dear, and soon I will come and free you from the evil that holds you enslaved," I explained. At that moment the moon came out from behind some clouds and I thought I saw a smile appear on her face, at least for a moment.

"Thank you, Great One, thank you," she said with happiness and relief in her voice.

She turned away and started down the mountain, her path revealed by the bright light of the full moon.

Great, I thought. *Now look at what you've got yourself into. Can't be happy with the way things are. You've just got to be a big hero. You can't cure all the evil in this world. You're not god; you're not even a man. And, now, what are you going to do? Battle the whole village?*

As a matter of fact, I was really terrified. What would happen if I was caught? My unusual appearance may allow for some surprise, but people have a way of destroying what they don't understand.

I figured that a simple plan would be best. Go to her house at night, take her and her son away, perhaps return to this cave or find another cave or leave the country completely. I do know that I should have sensed the urgency in her voice and gone the next night, but, and I don't know why I procrastinated, I waited three nights. It's the one decision I regret more than anything. I can look back and rationalize now, but it is just that: rationalization and making excuses; excuses for a great failure. After this episode I realized that I wasn't any better than all the humanity I had rejected. Bull or man, I was as much a total failure as all the men and women I had scorned.

What happened? Tragedy that I knew was coming, but ignored.

After three days I looked out from my cave at dawn, fully expecting to see the village below empty, as was typical for that time of day. Instead of this expected scene I saw people milling about, gathering in the town square. I had planned to go that night, rescue the woman and her child, and make our escape.

Curiosity got the best of me and, for the first time in years, I left my cave and made my way down the mountain. I was careful to stay hidden, but at the same time, I wanted to see what was going on. I reached a point above the village, probably about two hundred yards away, where I could see what was happening.

The villagers were lining up on either side of the central town square, leaving a long corridor in between. There was much noise and there was even singing that sounded a joyful note.

A celebration, no doubt. But, then I saw *her.* The same woman that had come to me for advice three nights before. She looked tired and her previously fine garments were torn and there were bruises on her face.

What's going on?

They led her to the end of the empty corridor. She appeared to be in a trance, stumbling along haphazardly. They left her standing alone as silence came over the crowd and all eyes turned towards her. I didn't see them at first, but I heard the sound, hoof beats, and men shouting. Then I saw them riding into the square. Men on horseback brandishing whips and sharp stakes. They rode fast, straight towards that defenseless victim. One after another rode by her and, as they rode by, they struck her with their whips and their stakes. They beat her, but she remained standing. The men rode back and started to make another pass through the human corridor. Finally, I came to my senses and realized what was transpiring and let out a yell and stood up. I saw many in the crowd look up at me and fingers point in my direction, but the men on horseback didn't stop. Once again they rode past and whipped her and stabbed at her and this time she crumpled to the ground.

By now I was bounding down the mountain to come to her aid. The crowd started to scream and there was a stampede of people trying to escape the wrath of the monster from the mountain. By the time I arrived, the only thing left in the town square was the bloody body of that poor woman. I didn't learn her name for many years. I ran to her and cradled her head in my arms as she looked up at me and, somehow, weakly smiled.

"What happened, dear child?" I asked.

She coughed and then she told me.

"He beat me again and when I fell to the ground he went into Mata's room. I couldn't let him hurt my child so I grabbed a knife from the kitchen and plunged it into his back..."

Before she could finish, her life passed away. I let out another roar as I cradled the lifeless body of this woman, a woman I barely knew, yet I knew all too well.

It's time to leave. Of that fact I had no doubt, but there was one loose end that needed to be addressed. A little boy. I had no idea where to look for her son. I didn't even know if the little boy was alive or was an innocent victim to all this carnage. I did know that the villagers would provide no help to my search and I also wasn't sure how I could care for a boy so young. Of course, I had done it previously, but that was a girl; boys were different.

Call it luck, or fate, or the will of the gods, because my search ended before it began. I heard soft footsteps and cries of, "Momma, Momma." I ducked into a shadow and the handsomest little boy I'd ever seen came running and then fell on top of the slain woman. Cries of "Momma, wake up... please wake up, Momma," mixed with loud sobs filled my ears and I crept out of the shadows.

"She's gone, Child. She did all she could to save you and now you are safe from the vicious fiend and she is at peace. Come with me and I will take care of you," I said softly, gently.

The lad looked up at me and stared into my eyes. There was no fear in his piercing, dark blue eyes, only sadness. As I watched the tears well up, I felt my own tears starting to flow. He had long black hair and was dressed in a simple white robe. I noticed that his arms, chest, and hands were covered with dried blood; his slain father's blood no doubt. I briefly speculated on how it came to stain his arms and hands in that particular way, but dismissed that thought immediately.

I knelt down and opened my arms wide and caught the poor child in a big hug as he ran to me. To this day I don't know how he could have trusted me so, but he adopted me right then and there. My heart was his as he clung to my chest and I held him tight. Finally, I relaxed my hold and he took my hand and led me to his house. Amazingly, not one of the village people made any attempt to find him or take him in. As I gathered all his belongings, I noticed the blood stained knife on the floor and the very small handprint that adorned its handle. I packed up as much as I could carry and we left. We went back to his mother and I carried her up into the mountains and buried her among the wild flowers. He cried and softly whispered, "Good-bye, Momma," and we left. I now had a new title: "Mother," a role I'd played once before.

27.

A T FIRST I WASN'T SURE where to go. I wanted to get far away from that village, but where would be a good and safe place to raise a little boy? We went west. I had fond memories of my carefree days in Africa and decided it was time to return. The journey wasn't particularly difficult; we had good weather the entire trip and I managed to find food and water. I had learned a few things over the many years I'd lived, one of which was how to travel great distances with few provisions. We crossed into India and made our way southwest, managed to find passage across the sea and eventually landed on the eastern shore of what would be modern day Ethiopia. From there we headed inland, to the jungle, to the place I'd lived before, only now instead of a blind girl, I was parent to a strong healthy boy. It wasn't long before I learned there was a big difference between boys and girls.

I found an area far away from any people and went to work building a shelter up in the trees. Mata was more monkey than boy, scooting up and down trees like a pro. He was adept at finding food and kept us well supplied with all sorts of fruit. I quickly learned to enjoy having a strong and resourceful boy for a companion. He grew quickly and was very bright. I made it my task to educate him and I started teaching him Latin, math, history (according to the Minotaur) and everything else I thought a boy should know.

Occasionally, we heard the drums of local natives and once in a while hunters from these tribes made it as far as our home. Our house was built up in a group of trees, shielded from view. Mata became very adept at tracking these hunters. He could be only ten feet away and they would be oblivious to his presence. He had an insatiable curiosity, asking question after question about other people, the world away from the jungle, history, God, and anything else he could think of. I did my best to answer him as honestly as I could, always trying to avoid prejudicing him (as I was) against humanity. He had genuine empathy for anything that seemed to be less fortunate than himself.

We had been living in the jungle for about two years when he asked me about his mother. I was surprised he hadn't asked earlier.

"What was she like?" he asked. "Was she pretty? Did she love me?"

"Mata, my dear boy, she loved you with all her heart. She did everything a mother could do to protect you. She gave her life."

"She was beautiful," he stated as a matter of fact. "I remember that. Her name was Popi. She was beautiful, but often sad. I wished I could make her happy. And when she smiled I felt my world fill with the light of her love."

I looked at him in amazement. Such astonishing words from such a young boy, such sensitivity.

"You are a remarkable young man, my Mata. Come now, it's time for another lesson."

I suppose he was attentive enough to my teaching, but all the while I knew that he wanted to be out exploring this new world, climbing trees, matching wits with panthers and snakes, learning from this world rather than merely hearing about it. I can't say that I blamed him. A three-thousand-year-old Minotaur must have seemed pretty boring compared to the raucous life of your average hippopotamus. But his mind was a sponge. Every sight, sound, and word was instantly engraved on his brain. It wasn't long before he knew everything there was to learn from me, from the jungle, from everything there was in the sky, on the ground, in the water. He was an amazing boy.

And he grew. Even though he was five years old when we left his homeland, he was tiny, more like a two-year-old. I don't know if it was the jungle freedom, or a diet heavy on bananas and honey, or just the expected growth spurt of a young boy, but he shot up almost overnight. Of course, he was never as big as me, but he was tall and straight and muscular, nimble like a monkey, capable of panther-like stealth, but strong and oh-so-smart. Not just book smart, but jungle smart.

He learned where snakes liked to hide and camouflage themselves, lying in wait for unsuspecting prey. He could spot them from high up in a tree; he'd then circle around to a vantage point a safe distance away and, just when the snake was about to strike an unsuspecting rodent, he'd swoop down and grab the creature around its neck. This saved the poor rat, but also made it impossible for the snake to fight back. Mata had powerful hands and he would effortlessly choke their life away.

I learned to skin snakes, cook snake meat, and make garments from multiple snake hides. I don't know why Mata disliked those snakes so much. I asked him once.

"Of all the animals, snakes are altogether evil. They have no purpose; I suppose they keep the rodent population down, but one rodent a month? Hardly what I would call effective pest control. They look demonic and they act demonic. Look what a snake did to Adam and Eve? The world would be a better place if it were rid of all such evil beasts."

I wasn't quite so sure, but I didn't think he would single-handedly rid the world of snakes, so I didn't belabor the point. I was pleased that he recalled some of my teaching, referring to his biblical reference.

I tell you these seemingly unimportant facts about Mata and snakes not to malign one of God's creations, rather to give you the proper perspective; to try to present to you the true nature of a boy who became a great and unsung hero.

I'm sure you've never heard of him. Mata does not appear in any history book, there's never been a made-for-TV movie about him, and I'm sure that I'm the only being that is aware that he even existed. At least up until now.

Back to the story.

We had been in the jungles of West Africa for about seven years. Mata was truly lord of those wild lands. The great cats avoided him, while monkeys and apes seemed to revere him as a great leader. He could commandeer a herd of elephants to do his bidding. Even the hippos—the most dangerous of beasts—seemed respectful of my young jungle boy. I'm sure you've all heard of Tarzan, the fictional ape man. Mata was everything Tarzan was supposed to be and more.

During those years we had almost no contact with other humans. We heard the drums of distant tribes fairly regularly, but rarely saw another man or woman for all those years. But all good things must come to an end and one day a hunting party stumbled into our corner of the world. Mata, who was a light-skinned Asian, was fascinated by the dark-skinned Africans. He heard them speak, but he couldn't understand their West African language. We spoke Latin, with a few German expletives thrown in once in a while. The boy couldn't help but play tricks on the unsuspecting tribesmen.

As the hunters crept up on their prey, Mata would let out the sound of a panther, alerting the gazelle or other quarry, and then laugh as the animal bounded away, leaving the men empty-handed. One time he caught two snakes, both especially large and both poisonous. This time he merely held them. I marveled at his strength and poise as he moved silently above the hunters and then released the two vipers, dropping them into the middle of their camp. My dear Mata let out quite the hyena laugh as the terrified men scurried for cover. Of course, I did my parenting duty and admonished the boy for playing such a trick, but inside I was far more proud than angry.

After a few days of tricks, Mata decided that those men had suffered enough. The wildebeest herd was only a few miles south. He managed to startle the herd leader and start him running directly towards the hunters' camp. Once the leader started to run, the rest of the herd followed and they headed straight for the hunters. Well, the rumbling grew louder and louder. I saw those men staring into the sky, looking for rain clouds that should have accompanied such thunder. Almost before it was too late they saw the great herd coming towards them. It was all they could do to scamper up trees to avoid being trampled. But once they found safety, they started shooting down on the passing beasts and ended up with an excellent tally for the day.

Hunters came regularly after that initial foray. Mata always did his best to help them out. After the first few times he would wave to them from a perch high up in one of the trees. They always smiled back and waved; I assumed they realized he was the cause of their good fortune.

After his first encounter Mata came to me looking perplexed.

"What's wrong, young man?" I asked, doing my best to seem like a concerned parent.

At first he shrugged his shoulders and didn't say anything, so I let it pass. However, an hour later he still seemed to be moping around, so I persevered.

"Come on, Mata. Tell me what's bugging you."

Finally, he answered.

"Those hunters, they had all sorts of tools to help them."

"You're right, knives, bows and arrows, spears. Weapons that help them hunt and can be used for far more sinister purposes."

He stared me in the eye and said, "Don't you think it would be good if we had weapons like those? I have to be careful to avoid lions or leopards. If had just a knife, I'm sure those beasts would be no match for me. I know they can be ferocious, but I'm a lot smarter."

I had hoped he would be spared humanity's natural tendency towards violence, but no such luck. And he was right. The jungle was a dangerous place for a boy like him. He was not an imposing Minotaur and that made him considerably more vulnerable to predators than me.

"OK," I replied, "You're one hundred percent correct. It would be safer for you to have at least a knife. Of course, I don't have the foggiest idea how to make one, so in that sense, you're on your own."

"I've got a pretty good idea of what to do," he answered and he ran off.

He was gone most of the day and didn't return until after dusk. I was starting to worry, but then I heard him coming; not just the rustling of the trees and bushes signaling his approach. I heard him whooping and howling, which was a bit unusual. I stared up into the trees, expecting him to drop down to the ground at any moment. Instead, I heard rustling directly above and then a loud thud directly in front of me. A slain leopard landed, followed by the triumphant Mata, brandishing his new knife and a length of rope.

"I did pretty good, don't you think?" he asked with a broad grin on his face.

"I'd say more than 'pretty good.' That leopard looks big and I'm sure he didn't just roll over and play dead for you. Let me see what you've built for yourself," I answered.

He handed me his knife. It was carved from ivory, honed to a razor sharp edge on one side and ending in a stiletto tip. The handle was also carved from the same ivory.

"I found the remains of one of the old elephants and used its tusk," he explained, "broke it down to size and then used a sharp rock to shape it. Then I found that if you beat those vines enough, you can get a lot of fine strong thread which I wove into this rope. Of course, when I finished I couldn't wait to try it out. This leopard obliged me. I guess I was careless because he was able to creep up on me and was ready to pounce when I heard him. I managed to get out of his way just in time, while slipping this noose around his neck. I pulled it tight and tied him to the tree branch. While he was fighting the rope, I jumped onto his back and plunged my knife into his neck. Pretty good, huh? It sure was an exhilarating experience, I just couldn't stop whooping and howling."

I looked at him and felt a twang of worry. The joy of the kill was something I could never understand, but I knew I didn't like it. I thought I'd be able to make him different, to make him better than the rest of humanity. It was at that moment that I realized there was nothing I could do to change human nature. Violence was ingrained and no amount of nurture or education could weed it out. Still, I decided, the boy was young and impressionable; there was a lesson to be learned.

"Why did you kill that poor beast, Mata?" I asked calmly and quietly.

He looked at me with a look of surprise and the exultation faded from his face.

"He… he was crouched right above me, I thought he was going to pounce."

"Could you have gotten away unharmed?"

He was silent for a moment and then looked down at his feet.

"I suppose so, but I wanted to see what I could do and try out my knife and rope..."

"...and now this leopard is dead. Leopards and other animals are not human. They attack and kill because they are beasts; they kill to eat or to protect themselves. But killing to prove that you can, even a vicious leopard, is not right. Where did the battle take place? Take me there."

We walked about two miles to the spot. There was still wet blood on the ground.

"Where was the leopard watching you? Show me the tree," I commanded.

He pointed to a spot only about ten feet away. I stopped and listened closely.

"Follow me," I ordered.

We walked about thirty yards away to a spot where the trees and brush were thick and then saw a small clearing. There was a bit of movement and then we both saw it at the same time. A baby leopard cub was softly purring and searching the area. Mata ran to it and picked it up as tears filled his eyes.

"This child is now yours," I stated and then turned to walk home.

Mata trailed behind me the entire way, silently; the only noise was the occasional purr or soft growl from the leopard cub.

Lesson taught, I reflected as a smile formed on my lips.

We, or rather I should say, Mata, became the proud parent of a baby female leopard. I have to admit, he took the responsibility to heart and treated that leopard like a queen. Luckily, the little lady—that's actually what he named her, Lady—was weaned and feeding her was not a problem. Mata's hunting skills improved with the help of his new tools and he became an entity worthy of respect. I think he was about twelve at this time and, although he wasn't huge, he was big enough, nimble and crafty. He could do things that I never even dreamed possible for a man.

He could look at a bush and determine if a lion had passed recently, or walk along the ground and tell me if there was an impala nearby. Sometimes we'd walk together and he would suddenly jump and catch a low lying branch without making a sound. I'd be walking along, talking with the boy, and then turn to the side to see that he'd slipped away a hundred yards back and was stalking a water buffalo. He could move silently through the underbrush or from tree to tree, sometimes incredibly fast.

But he'd also learned his lesson. Never again did he kill wantonly. Oh, he still hunted, but he would only kill what he needed for food. Sometimes he was forced to defend himself and he always emerged victorious. And he cared for Lady and me. Lady grew quickly and it wasn't long before they were hunting side-by-side. Now, *there* was a formidable duo. You may talk about Batman and Robin, or Sherlock Holmes and Watson, or Simon and Garfunkel, but Mata and Lady truly struck fear into and commanded the respect of all the denizens of the jungle.

They, on the other hand, were always respectful. They did hunt, a necessary evil while living in the wild, at least for humans and leopards, but they were never bullies. When the village hunting parties came around, they were always treated to a fresh antelope or wildebeest, courtesy of Mata and Lady. If danger lurked, the warning cry rose from Mata's powerful lungs.

As for me, I became the wise old counselor, content to stay in our home built in the trees, eat the fare that my young charge gathered, and stroll along the ground. I imparted to Mata all the knowledge and bit of wisdom I'd learned through the ages, right or wrong. I taught him about love, justice, responsibility, and restraint. I told him about music and books, taught him to read and write Latin and German along with his native language. I recited some of the great stories of antiquity, Homer, Aristophanes, Socrates, the Bible. He was an apt pupil when I could convince him to stay and listen. Despite his frequent forays into the jungle, he always gave me the greatest respect and there was never a moment I wasn't proud of him.

Of course, it couldn't last, nothing ever does. It was the slave traders that destroyed what we had built together.

Mata noticed it first. The native hunting parties stopped coming around. They had been coming on a more or less monthly basis for years, but then over a period of three months and during prime hunting season, they didn't appear. I, for one, was happy to have more peace and quiet, but Mata felt a bit unsettled, causing him and Lady to go off and investigate. What he found filled him with anger and resolve.

The native villagers had been rounded up and were locked away in cages. Men with strange weapons, muskets, stood guard. The men, women, and children penned up were full of fear and some openly wept. The village was nearly empty of all its inhabitants, only the very old and the very young were not imprisoned. Men with muskets patrolled everywhere, some black, some white.

Mata channeled his anger into action. First, he gathered up two of the more deadly snakes that roamed the jungle and managed to carry them back to the village. It was nightfall and most of the men were inside, only the guards remained outdoors and there were two of them, one guarding the penned up villagers and the other outside the tent where the unwanted elderly and babies were housed. From a long tree branch that extended out over the area, Mata could creep out almost directly over them.

Silently, he dropped the snakes down on his unsuspecting quarry. Loud screams followed and the guards raced away, each with a very poisonous snake wrapped around their neck or torso. Mata then simply dropped to the ground and released all the captives and led them away into the jungle. The entire village, or what was left of the villagers, escaped. Mata, always curious, returned the next morning to see the slave trader's reaction. Needless to say, there were shouts of anger and much finger pointing. Some of the men searched for the wayward guards, who were discovered a few hundred yards away, both very ill, suffering from the poison of the snake bites. The other men, in their great anger, shot the two guards dead rather than try to save them, then they burned the village to the ground and left.

The villagers moved to a new spot and started rebuilding their world, a world which now included a fear that had been unknown a few days before. Mata, to his credit, declared war on the slave trade. He had heard the men talking German and realized that those that were captured were destined to live a life in bondage. He knew about slavery from my teaching and he certainly remembered how cruel men could be towards each other. He and Lady turned their talents towards fighting this evil, bringing a reign of terror that frightened the invaders away for months at a time. But the villains always returned, usually with more men and more cruelty.

At first, all it took was a few well-placed snakes or a trail of sweet honey to entice some of the ferocious ant colonies into the slave trader's beds. Then, Mata became bolder. He would send Lady bounding through the camp, startling and frightening the inhabitants and then he would saunter in and release any captives. Sometimes, he would create a different type of diversion, a fire or something and then overpower any stragglers. I think he and Lady, along with the help of a few snakes and nasty insects, saved several thousand native Africans from lives destined for oblivion.

He became greatly revered among the native crowd and I think he let it go to his head, because he also grew careless, believing he was invincible. Of course, I was never much help to him and, wisely, he never asked for my assistance. I think he decided that I was far too passive for such dangerous affairs and that I would probably be more hindrance to his endeavors than help.

The troubles started with one of his "attacks" on the slave traders' encampment. On this occasion he sent Lady charging into the camp, the plan being to create the usual diversion so that Mata could then follow and release the imprisoned men and women. They had done the same thing dozens of times before, always without a hitch. Unfortunately, the slave traders were either getting smarter or they just got lucky.

Normally, the camps were protected by various traps and there were always sentries posted around the perimeter. Mata's jungle-trained senses always discerned the guards' locations and all the traps and he and Lady easily avoided them. This time Lady was caught. It wasn't one of the traps or a guard; it was a weak tree limb. Lady climbed out on the limb, preparing to leap into the middle of the encampment, when the limb cracked, alerting the sentry that something was afoot. When Lady finally pounced all eyes were already trained in her direction and there was no surprise, only gunfire and she was felled. Mata, of course, was watching from his vantage point in another tree and, when he saw the men converging on poor helpless Lady, he couldn't help himself. He raced to her side and overpowered several of the guards, but a fifteen-year-old lad is no match for thirty full grown men with firearms. Mata was quickly overpowered and bound. Lady passed away, a true heroine, responsible for saving a multitude of lives.

Mata's fate was not nearly as pleasant. Let me preface this by saying that anyone that would stoop to making money from the buying and selling of humanity is lower than the lowest slime. Someone who knowingly rips families apart, packs human beings like sardines in filthy cargo holds, and ships them off to lives of bondage is just pure evil. What they did to Mata was worse than evil. I'd seen Roman crucifixion, primitive forms of torture and such, but my poor Mata suffered so much more.

All the time I really had no idea what was happening. Mata and Lady went off together almost every day and rarely informed me. Mata would tell me later and, like a good Dad, I worried, but he was his own man and didn't listen to me anyway. But when he didn't return, not just that night, but also the next, I became worried and I set out to find the two of them.

I wasn't exactly sure where to start, but I figured slave traders would set up camp towards the coast, so I headed in that direction. It took me a couple of days, but I finally heard some shouts and gunfire and followed the noise to their camp. What I saw made me sick. First I found Lady, outside the camp, rotting, covered with flies. I knew it was she because of the heart-shaped spot on her rump which was still visible. I buried her where I'd found her, tears filling my eyes, but, at that moment, I was even more terrified for Mata.

Terror wasn't the right word. Fear, which turned to hatred and anger, filled my heart. There, in the camp, was Mata, spread eagled, tied by his hands and feet between two trees. He was bleeding and burned and torn, but still breathing. The men were taking turns using him for target practice, branding him with white hot irons, slashing and cutting all different parts. Only one finger remained on his left hand, they were all gone from the right, all his toes were gone, and there was a deep slash across his abdomen and his back.

Now, it is true that I was never much of a fighter, but I knew that I could fill men's hearts with fear and with the proper motivation I could play the part of the ferocious monster to the max. Well, there's no doubt that I had the motivation. I stood up as straight as I could and let out a loud, continuous roar. I rattled the bushes and threw rocks and branches into the camp. Then I charged into the camp, first on all fours and then I stood up, bearing my teeth, continuing my monstrous roars.

The show was enough to scare of all the native help; only the few actual slave traders stood their ground. They briefly raised their muskets, but they were shaking so much that they couldn't even fire a single shot. I bounded towards them and they didn't have any stomach to engage in a brawl with a demon; they followed their hired help in flight. I suddenly found myself alone in the camp, that is, only Mata and I remained. I raced to his side and gently cut him down. I cradled his mangled body in my arms and carried him away. There were no prisoners at that moment, so I did not have to bother with releasing any captive natives. My final act was to torch the camp. There were several fires burning and I set several torches ablaze and burned their tents and all their possessions to the ground, hoping to send a final message. Then I left, carefully carrying poor Mata, still feeling his shallow breath as his chest moved up and down against mine.

We finally reached home and I ever so carefully and gently laid him on one of our mats. He opened his eyes and smiled, and then he coughed, a big clot of blood.

"I guess I should have been more careful," he said softly, his voice weak and raspy.

"Don't try to talk, you need to save all your strength," I answered.

"It's better this way. Better for me and for you. I'll get to be with Lady and my mother and with Him. And you won't have to worry. I'll be safe, safe forever," he said, his voice fading.

"Don't talk like that. You'll be up and running around in no time. I'll help you just like I helped old Nebuchadnezzar."

I held him to my chest and I felt his last breath and then he was dead.

I let out a loud, long roar and felt the urge for vengeance. For the first time in my life I wanted to kill those men. I found the feeling frightening and I wasn't sure what to do, so I simply sat there, holding my dear, sweet, heroic Mata. Day turned to night and then to day again and finally I let the poor boy go. I buried him next to Lady. My thirst for vengeance passed and I spent several months contemplating what I should do next. The slave traders never returned to that area. The sad irony wasn't lost on me. All of Mata's amazing exploits had not stopped such evil from coming, but my single tirade created such fear that the surrounding country, for a distance of a hundred miles at least, was safe for years and years.

28.

FTER MATA I FELL INTO the deepest despair I had ever felt in all my years. I left the Dark Continent and made my way back to Europe. I never really settled anywhere. I wandered through Italy and Germany, spent some time among a herd of cows in the Swiss Alps, hid out in some mountainous caves for a time, wandered north to Finland, and even went to Greece. I thought about visiting Crete, but times were changing and being such an unusual beast limited my freedom. I don't know how many years I wasted wandering about.

I watched Napoleon march across Europe, suffer defeat in Russia, and finally lose out forever. I saw kings, queens, popes, and armies all come and go, never taking any interest; my heart held nothing but contempt for humans and cows. Finally, after decades and decades of aimless wandering, I came to England. It was purely by chance that I ended up there, the result of a violent storm and luck (or misfortune depending on one's viewpoint).

It was the early 1890's and I was living among a herd of cows on the coast of France. During the day I tended to stay in the field and try to make some time with some of the Elsies, almost always unsuccessfully. At night, when the herd headed home, I'd hide out among the trees or bushes. One particular night there was a violent storm with heavy rain, fierce winds, and lightning. I was looking for a place of safety and I ducked under a heavy tarp in the back of a wagon which I found parked in the barn on the farm.

It was pretty late and I fell asleep. The next thing I knew the cart was hooked up to a team of horses and I was on my way to the coast. I'd planned to duck out at my first opportunity, but much to my surprise the whole team of horses and the wagon plodded up a ramp onto a cargo ship headed across the Channel. Like it or not, I was on my way to England.

The cargo ship docked in London and my wagon and horses were unloaded, along with a large number of pine boxes. The wagon was left alone for a short time and I used the opportunity to slip away and find a hiding place in a dark alleyway filed with rotting garbage. I spent the day shooing away rats and when night fell, I wandered out into the city, staying in the shadows.

I marveled at how humanity had progressed. London was huge, filled with more people than I'd ever seen in such a small area. It was also incredibly dirty. Everywhere I went there were piles of garbage with rats running here and there. A foul stench filled the air and most of the people looked as if they hadn't bothered to bathe in years. The streets were lit up in many areas by lamps and carriages of all types raced back and forth over the stone streets. Once in a while someone managed to get a glimpse of me and I'd hear a scream or shout. I knew I needed to find a place to hide out before daybreak or else I might be in more than a little bit of trouble.

As it turned out, providence was with me, or so I thought at the time. It started with a gang of young hooligans, boys probably fourteen or fifteen years old. One of them saw me lurking in the shadows and let out a loud scream. Well, before I had time to say, "Send me to Crete," they were after me. There must have been twenty of them, each carrying a large club or stick, and a few had knives. I was not inclined to see my immortal ways end on such a note so I took off as fast as I could. I had about a hundred yards head start, but I knew that eventually I'd be cornered. As I ran I tried opening several of the doors that lined the back streets of that part of London. My luck held out and I was able to round a corner and duck into a darkened doorway. I gave the doorknob a twist and fell into an even darker room. My would-be assassins ran right past as I counted my good fortune. I planned to hide out only until I was sure I was safe, but after only a few minutes the resident of that dwelling appeared.

I was up against the wall in the darkened room when I heard the doorknob start to turn. I stood behind the door, trying in vain to make myself small and inconspicuous. A man came in and lit the table lamp. He was dressed in a dark coat with his hat pulled down low on his head. He was a burly man with broad shoulders. He turned and saw me almost immediately, but surprisingly, he didn't scream or run away or do anything. All he did was stare. The silence was more than I could bare and I started to speak, babble sort of meaningless words to try to prove to this stranger that I was not some sort of monster to be feared or a freak escaped from the circus. He raised his hand, gesturing for me to stop.

"Calm down, relax," he said. "I've seen worse, almost every day, as a matter of fact." And, he let out a little chuckle and offered me the only chair in that small room.

"Tell me your name, Brute," he requested, well, more like commanded.

"Minotaur, I'm the Minotaur famed of legend and myth," I answered, feigning modesty.

"Never heard of you, Brute, and Minotaur is far too hard of a name to remember, so from now on I'll call you Brutus, Brute for short. I'm John, John Carver, but most everyone calls me John the Butcher."

"Why do they call you that, if you don't mind me asking?"

"Butcher isn't exactly the most proper term, Brute. Technically, I'm a meat cutter. Butchers only work on the meat after I've cut it down to size for them. Me, I take those big carcasses of cows and sheep and such and I cut away all the stuff nobody wants, trim it, get the carcass down to a size so that all the fine steaks and roasts are easily accessible and then the butcher comes in. But to the ignorant world, I'm just a butcher."

In the pale light I was able to see the stains on the apron fastened around his neck and I realized that it was blood.

"I'm not sure I want to stay here with a butcher, excuse me, meat cutter. I'm sure you've..."

"Noticed that you look like a bull? Hard to miss it, Brute. But don't worry. I've seen much worse, far more devious, monstrous beings than you. There's evil in this world; evil that will destroy us all if we let it. But, no worry; it's out there in the night. It would not dare to come in here."

We shook hands and then spent some time fixing up a space for me to sleep. The room was pretty good size, about twenty by twenty, and had everything necessary to make it a comfortable, functional living space. There was a corner with a stove for cooking, a table, one chair, John's bed, and a passage that led to a communal water closet. John had a soft mat rolled up in the corner and he lay this in the corner for me.

"A royal bed," I commented. For me this wasn't far from the truth, having spent years sleeping on makeshift beds that varied from rock to ice to trees.

John prepared dinner and, while we ate, I told him my story. The tale kept him enthralled and it was well past dawn when I finished and he announced he needed to get some sleep. I realized that I was more than exhausted and I passed out as soon as my head hit the mat. It was dark again when I awoke and Jack was gone. Thus began my existence as a true night owl.

I suppose it was by necessity that I almost never ventured out during daylight. Times had changed and, outside of a circus, a being such as me would certainly cause considerable consternation and commotion. Half-human beasts simply were not a part of proper society anymore. I learned to keep to the dark alleyways and to keep away from almost all people. That's not to say I didn't make some acquaintances. There were feral dogs and cats, one particularly large rat I called Mobus and, occasionally, some of the people of the night: prostitutes, winos, petty thieves; the "dregs" of society who didn't seem to care if I was a human, a bull, or their fairy Godmother.

I would not call 1890's London paradise. The streets were lined by piles of garbage and there were piles of horse manure every few feet. A thick blanket of black soot, courtesy of the coal-fired furnaces of the day, covered almost everything, including the people. And then there was the smell; the combination of raw human sewage, horse manure, rotting garbage and a great unwashed mass of humanity created a foul stench that filled the air. It didn't matter if one lived in White Chapel or Buckingham Palace; the pungent scent found you and followed everywhere. I think it was necessary to go a day's ride outside the city to find clean fresh air.

I settled into a routine or sorts. I slept from just after sunup until late afternoon. I would arise, attend to all the necessary personal chores, tidy up the room, and then prepare a meal for John. I developed into a pretty good chef, able to make a variety of delectable meals, blending the paucity of meat and vegetables that John brought home in imaginative ways that were surprisingly palatable. John and I would talk after dinner and then he would read for a while.

We talked about the world around us, my experiences through the years, and life in "modern" London.

"I don't know how I found my way into the meat-cutting business," he told me. "One day I was staring into the butcher shop at all the fine cuts of meat and the next thing I knew I was talking with the clerk, who sent me around to the butcher, who gave me the address of the slaughterhouse, and I became a cutter. I seemed to have a natural aptitude for such work. It wasn't long before I was the head meat cutter. I suppose if I'd made my way to the hospital I would have been a surgeon. Not much difference between the two, except meat cutters need to be a bit more precise."

"Perhaps you're right about that. From what I've seen, doctors and surgeons seem to make things worse far more often than they actually help," I answered.

"It's all such a dirty business, if you want to know the truth. Those carcasses just hanging there, blood dripping down, entrails cast into the corner, festering until someone sees fit to clean it all up. And how is it cleaned? Just scoop it all up, throw it into a large bin, and put it outside to let it rot some more, attract rats and roaches; one more item to foul the air. London is a decaying city. Nothing but garbage, rot, sewage, and blight. And not just in the piles on the street; there's also the human refuse. Thieves, whores, opium addicts, swindlers, whores. They tear at a man's soul, they do!" He was almost raving now, his voice rising, his nostrils flared, his eyes shining brightly in the candlelit room.

His passion fascinated me. I encouraged him to continue and he obliged.

"So here we are, you and me, living in this one room in the middle of all this filth and corruption. Just run away you might say, move to the country away from it all, but that wouldn't be right. Who would be the protector, who would save us from ourselves? No, it's best to stay, to wait for the right time, and then end it all. Eliminate the danger and make the world a safer, cleaner place for young men and boys."

"What about Minotaurs?" I inquired, not wanting to be left out. "And girls and women? Shouldn't they be saved, too?"

"Women? You mean harlots. If there were a way to reproduce without getting the 'fairer sex' involved the world would be a far better place, less pain, less heartache. But as for you, you're OK. I think a world full of the likes of you would be simply tremendous."

"Well, thank you for that," I said. I really wanted to hear more of his thoughts, but he'd gone silent. He was staring at his hands, his meat cutter hands. He was holding a knife, a long shiny, very sharp knife. The blade reflected the candle light creating an eerie pattern on the ceiling, giving the room a bizarre sense of the macabre.

"Enough of my ranting, it's bedtime," he announced.

It was around ten, his usual bedtime and as soon as he hit the pillow, I headed out into the night, which was my normal routine.

Sometimes all I would do was wander along the dark alleyways, smiling at the dogs and cats and rats. Usually, I would stop at Rosie's to buy a few vegetables and some fruit. Rosie was a sweet old lady, almost eighty and nearly blind. I suppose that's why my startling appearance didn't seem to faze her. I once asked her about that and she stared at me and then said:

"Quint, my eyesight's not nearly as bad as you think. You may look like the most fearsome, vicious beast that ever walked this earth, but that doesn't matter. It's what we look like inside that counts; it's our heart, our soul that makes a man or woman. And you've got a heart of solid gold. It's too bad, though. Such as you end up beaten down and destroyed. That's the way of this world. Sad, but true."

I loved old Rosie. I stopped at her stand every night for almost a year. I loved the fruit and her wisdom, but most of all, I loved her for her acceptance.

Life went on and I was fairly content. That is, I was content until I saw *him*. How many years had passed and he was still alive. At first I wasn't sure. I mean, how could he still be around almost six hundred years later? Maybe I was mistaken. I'd only caught a quick glimpse as he rode by in a carriage, a truly handsome carriage, pulled by four fine horses. But it was him, no question, and I was sure he had seen me. It was my old friend, or nemesis, Vlad, now also known as Count Dracula.

He was definitely older, appeared to be in his fifties, a touch of gray in his hair and a thin white moustache. I couldn't be sure if Renfield was with him, but it certainly wouldn't have surprised me. I was sure that "The Count" had seen me. Even in that brief moment I clearly saw him tip his fancy top hat towards me. At the time I surmised, correctly I might add, that my blood had kept him alive all through the years. I was also sure that I could expect a visit from him, or one of his minions, before too long.

But for the time being I was safe. After all, he would have to find me in that labyrinth of back-alleyways, dark and dank old tenements, and the unwashed members of a society that preferred to ignore the social ills that permeated the day. I trimmed my horns and donned a hood as I had done during my monastery days. A few of my casual acquaintances questioned this new look, but most just shrugged their shoulders and went about business as usual. I went out only when I absolutely had to and then I returned to that little room as quickly as I could.

Maybe he didn't really see me; maybe he'll leave me alone; maybe he's finished his business in London and has already departed, gone back to his castle in Transylvania.

But it wasn't to be. I came home early one morning and saw the light on under the door. I wasn't surprised when I went in and found "The Count" sitting on a chair with Renfield crouching down in the corner. We now had two chairs in the room and I sat down opposite Vlad as he stared into my eyes. The sinister look hadn't changed, only now all I saw was evil, no hatred, no look of gratitude for the long life he'd lived thanks to me and my blood; nothing but evil. He was staring at the little vial that he had worn around his neck for all these years. It was completely empty.

"You're a hard beast to find, old friend," he began in a very soft clear voice. "Believe me I know, because I've been searching for almost two hundred years. I learned about your years in the monastery, but I couldn't bring myself to go there and, at that time, there wasn't any need. But, then you just vanished. I'm sure you can imagine how that made me feel."

He lightly tapped his fingers on the table, staring into my eyes, his voice never wavering, never rising, only that steady, annoying, superior, quiet voice. I could feel my hair starting to stand on end as anger welled up inside.

He continued on, "Look at this little vial. There's not one little flake of dried blood inside. The truth is that it's been empty now for almost twenty five years. Just look at poor, wretched Renfield. He's almost all dried up. All his flies and beetles have done nothing for him and your blood's been gone for so long. Do you really want to see him withered away and dead?"

"Listen 'Count Dracula,' " I started to say, but he held up his hand and stopped me.

"No, my dear Minotaur, you listen. You don't understand all that I do for this world. You see me as a vicious, evil monster. You are a fine one to see others in such a light. But, I do incredibly vital work among those whom I meet. I help them in ways you could never understand, help them fulfill their dreams and goals. For example, your roommate, John. He has such thoughts and ideas in his head, noble, valuable notions that would never reach fruition but for my assistance. With your help, I've helped hundreds just like him; helped them achieve greatness, fame, and fortune. Do you want to be responsible for allowing such benevolence to fade out of existence?

"And, my dear old friend, we don't like this completely unnecessary decay. It would take such a small gesture on your part to help us. I am more than willing to offer just compensation for your trouble. And I only want enough to fill up three or four of these little vials. Is that truly worth quibbling about?"

Was he right? Was it really worth fussing over? What did I know about him anyway? A lot can happen in six hundred years. Of all people in this world, I knew that to be true. But I sensed something extraordinarily evil within him, something that should be allowed to die, almost as if Satan himself was sitting across from me and asking for my soul. I'd had the same feeling before, in a dream.

"No and No and No!" I screamed. "Not for Renfield and definitely not for you!"

I stood and reached for him across the table, wrapping my hand around his throat, lifting him out of his chair.

"It would be better for the world if I gave nature a bit of help and ended your wretched life now," I said, a bit more calmly, while still holding the Count tightly by the throat.

It was at that moment that his chair came crashing down on my arm. Unlike so many famous movie scenes, the chair did not shatter into a thousand tiny bits of wood. Instead, it nearly broke my arm and made me release the fiend, who quickly took a step back. Renfield stood at his side.

"It is unfortunate that we could not come to a peaceful agreement, but no matter. I'll seek for alternatives. In the meantime, the sun is nearly up and I do abhor bright sunshine. Good Day, Minotaur. I trust you will not allow our little differences to come between us."

He held out his hand, but I stood unmoved and glanced towards the door. He and Renfield silently exited. I sat down to ponder what would come next. I sensed the desperation in his voice, beneath the façade of refinement.

Maybe I should have just given him what he wanted. It wouldn't mean much to me, a few drops of blood. There was a sense of fear about him, fear of death and the unknown. Such a feeling was so very different from my own. We had both lived unnaturally long lives, but for me death was something that would almost be welcome, freeing me from the despair of this world. Vlad seemed to cling to his miserable life. Perhaps the fear of the unknown was more than he could tolerate. I didn't know.

John came in at that moment. I wondered where he had been all night. He looked disheveled and I saw blood on his apron.

"Working the night shift?" I inquired, but he didn't say a word, just sat down, and put his face on his hands. He looked exhausted. I helped him up, washed some blood from his hands, and helped him into bed. Whatever had happened, he wasn't saying and it had taken some sort of toll on my benefactor.

29.

THE NEXT DAY THERE WAS a great buzz throughout the neighborhood. There had been a murder; not the run of the mill clean simple stabbing or shooting that was common to this part of London. This was a particularly gruesome slaying—a prostitute brutally stabbed and then mutilated. I was glad that it wasn't anyone I knew as I was familiar with many of the "Ladies of the Night." I didn't think twice about it as I lay down to sleep. As usual, John had already gone to work.

The next night I stopped to visit with Rosie. She was very hyped up about the previous night's murder. Personally, I didn't understand it, but this is what she said.

"It was the work of the Devil, if you ask me, or one of his evil demons. Maggie told me that Mary Ann was with three men just an hour before they found her. One was dressed all fancy, but it was dark and she couldn't tell anymore. But mark my words, it was Satan that caused it all and it'll happen again."

I smiled at her, thanked her for the free apples, and went on my way. I made it home earlier than usual and saw John before he left for work.

"You're back early tonight," he observed. "The night people all stayed in?"

"Everyone's a bit rattled by that murder the other night. It's no big deal to me. Life is cheap in these parts; I don't know what's so special about Mary Ann Nichols."

"That was her name?" he asked, rhetorically. "One less blight in the night. One less whore to tempt unsuspecting young men and boys. White Chapel's better off."

"She was a person, John. I'm sure she didn't choose to live the harlot's life. People've got to survive the best they can. I don't think anyone has the right to feel superior. Look at you, carving up the carcasses of dead animals. Is that any more righteous than selling one's only possession, one's own body, to put food on the table?"

"Eh, you talk like there's no victim in the crime. Perhaps you are correct when you say it's her body to do with as she pleases, but there are victims, Brute. The men and boys she defiles, the diseases she spreads, the wives of her victims, mothers and sisters all ignored. These whores are nothing but a menace, flaunting themselves and mocking everything that makes society decent."

The venom in his words surprised me, but I held my tongue. John had been very good to me and I was sure it was all just words. But then it happened again, only worse. Eight days later Annie Chapman was found dead, her throat slashed and her abdomen cut open. This one hit a little closer to home. I'd met Annie several times. She was always very pleasant, never even flinched at my unusual appearance, and always had a sweet hello when I'd pass her on the street. And John didn't come home at all that night.

I went to see Rosie again and she told me the same story. Three hours before they found poor Annie she had been seen with three men, one elderly, one finely dressed in a cloak and top hat and the third with dirty blonde hair, stocky and wearing a leather apron. My suspicions were aroused when I thought about the recent visit of Vlad and Renfield and John's typical attire. And he was well-versed in dismembering cows and sheep and chickens. He did commonly wear a leather apron, had dirty blonde hair and a stocky build. And

Vlad was usually seen in a cloak and top hat, and Renfield was definitely elderly. But then I thought surely it's just coincidence that John came home stained with blood the night of the first murder or that he didn't come home at all the second night or that Vlad was able to locate me so quickly after our paths briefly crossed that one night. All just coincidence... or was it?

Perhaps it will all just go away. Perhaps John's anger towards women in general and prostitutes in particular were just empty words, perhaps... There were too many "ifs" and "perhaps" to be coincidence. Then nothing happened for a few weeks. John went back to his usual routine and there were no more murders. No word from dear old Vlad either. I began to lay my fears and conjecture aside and went back to my old routine. John was quieter than usual, came home in the evening, ate in silence, and went to bed as soon as the sunset. Something was wrong, but I was afraid to ask; afraid that my suspicions were silly and only the result of my own paranoia.

Of course, the papers had a heyday with the "White Chapel" murders and "Jack the Ripper." That's what he was eventually called. Initially, he was dubbed "Leather Apron" and this name sent shivers through me.

It was after the next two murders that I became convinced that I was living with a deranged mass murderer. It was three weeks later and John didn't come home again, not until dawn on Sunday morning. His hands, apron, trousers, and shoes were drenched in blood. I asked him point blank and he said they had made him work late, there was a quota to meet and everyone had been working nonstop through the night. But a few hours later the news of two more grisly murders hit the streets.

I decided to take a different approach with John. When he awoke, at about three that afternoon I fixed him some tea and shared it with him, which was a bit unusual for me, not being much of a tea drinker.

"Isn't it a shame, all these gruesome murders?" I asked, waiting to see some response. I continued, "It won't be safe for anyone to go out after dark with the likes of this insane 'Jack the Ripper' out there. I can tell you that the 'night people' are a little on edge."

"If they aren't whores I don't think they'll have anything to worry about. Those wretched tarts deserved what they got. It could have been worse, should have been worse."

He stared down into his now empty teacup.

"Would you like another cup?" I asked, innocently.

He responded with a grunt which I took as a yes and I refilled his cup.

"I have no right to judge anyone, well, maybe some right. After all, I've been alive for a few thousand years," I added. "But, if you want my opinion, I hope that they find this beast and sentence him to be hanged, shot, and then locked away for life. Nobody deserves to be treated the way these poor women have been treated and I'm not talking about just the four that were murdered. Do you think a woman chooses such a life? How many little girls sit on their daddy's knee and say, 'Daddy, when I'm old enough I want to be a whore'? I think the solution to the injustice in this world is to take pity on those that are less fortunate, like you did for me, and give them a life with dignity."

John smiled at my little speech. "You should run for Parliament, Brute. That's the place for speeches. But it wouldn't matter. Such women have been around almost as long as the world's been in existence. Now, be still. I don't want to talk about such things anymore. It makes me sick to my stomach."

He sat in silence for about an hour and then left to wash before disappearing into the streets. I still had my suspicions and decided to try to follow him. I really had no idea where he might have gone and it wasn't night yet. I put on my "monk" disguise and went out into the bustling streets, doing my best to remain inconspicuous—a futile task. Everywhere I went the disheveled and unwashed pointed and stared; some kids threw rocks and it was, all in all, a very unpleasant experience.

There's a vicious monster loose in White Chapel and all they can do is point and stare and treat me like a monster. But, who was I kidding? I was a monster, at least to them. They weren't all Rosies or even John Carvers. I guess I can't blame them. I was a monster; a freak of nature who belonged in the sideshow of a carnival.

To Hell with them. They deserve whatever they get. And I went home, angry at the ignorance of humanity and angry with myself. One thing I was sure of, however, there would be another murder.

I changed my strategy. Everything seemed to return to normal. John went to work, came home at the usual time, ate dinner, talked a bit, and then went to bed at his usual time of ten o'clock. I went out as usual and life went on. However, when I went out I waited. I'd stand in the darkened alley across the street, staking out my own room. Day after day I waited and nothing happened. Finally, about six weeks later, I saw John leave at about midnight. There was the usual light mist in the air and I was able to tail him fairly inconspicuously. I wore a black cloak and blended into the night.

It wasn't long before my patience was rewarded. John met with a well-dressed man and his elderly companion, clearly Vlad and Renfield. They were standing under a street lamp and soon a very heated discussion began.

"You promised, you promised!" he screamed. "Nothing's changed, they're still out there. One a month isn't enough. And that brute; when does he go? You want his blood? Just say the word and you'll have a gallon, enough to keep us alive for a thousand years."

"Such short-sightedness, *Jack*. One mustn't settle too lightly. Eternity is in our grasp," Vlad calmly observed. "But, there is the task at hand; another young lady to satisfy your lust for justice and to feed myself and poor Renfield. The blood, the human organs do so satisfy, and you are such a skilled cutter, Jack. Now take us to our next sacrifice."

The three left together and I followed, keeping a safe distance. The fog was growing thicker and it was harder to see them. It was a quiet night, however, and I could hear their footsteps up ahead. All of a sudden, the night became still, nothing but fog and silence. The faint illumination from the street lamps actually made things worse. I quickened my pace until I heard a scream and I raced toward the sound. I found the three of them: John hunched over the body, performing gruesome surgery on the dead woman, Vlad standing beside him, salivating, exhorting him to hurry, and Renfield cowering in a corner, away from the grisly scene, waiting for the bit of liver or kidney that was to be thrown his way.

It was more than I could take. I raced into the pale light and grabbed John around the throat. He lunged at me with his long, sharp blade, but I held him at arm's length. He had a wild look in his eyes as my hands tightened around his neck. He stared at Vlad for help, but the evil one was crouched on the ground, biting at the fallen woman like a vicious wolf. I held John until the life had been squeezed out of him and then picked up his knife. Vlad looked up with a wild look that filled me with hatred and loathing. I plunged the blade into his back and he went limp as blood pooled around him. I left Renfield to himself; he was rendered harmless now and I could tell his days were numbered.

I took John's knife and walked away, tossing the knife in the Thames. The next day I heard of the murder, but no mention of John or Vlad or Renfield. Was it some sort of cover-up, or had Renfield managed to clean up the scene? I never learned the truth. I did read an unusual obituary a few weeks later about an unidentified elderly man found dead in a room at one of the finer hotels. It was unusual because the cause of death was starvation. Without his master, poor Renfield was helpless, but he had lived over six hundred years.

I had carried out an act of justice. Still, the police came knocking on my door one night, perhaps looking for me or my now-departed roommate. I wasn't at home at the time, luckily, because, if I had been home, I'm sure I would be languishing in a prison somewhere. I suppose I *was* guilty of murder. In all my thousands of years on this earth, John and Vlad were the only two people I ever killed, and I barely consider Vlad to be a person. Vlad had released the latent evil in John. An evil that, I believe, exists in all of humanity. There was no choice but to end his life. He would have gone on, killing and killing and killing more in his vain attempt to rid the world of prostitutes that he considered to be a blight on human dignity. I suppose I'm rationalizing when I say that it was Vlad who destroyed John. I guess that's the human part of me.

I went to Rosie's fruit stand and found a young woman working. I asked where Rosie was and she told me she was gone. She didn't show up one day, which surprised all the usual night owls. They sent a girl around to her room and there they found her dead and stiff as a board. Such is life. One day vibrant and full, and the next day fertilizer.

I decided it was time to leave London. I managed to find night passage on a ship across the channel and made my way to France. To Paris and the start of a new life. A life among the best and brightest of the day.

30.

I DIDN'T START MY LIFE in turn-of-the-century France cavorting with all the unknown, future celebrities. I didn't even go to Paris at first. I stopped in the countryside and settled in among the French bovine crowd. Unlike their human counterparts, the cows didn't sport berets, spend their days smoking cigarettes in the cafés, or their nights creating masterful works of art. They were just cows, like the cows of Switzerland or Germany or Babylon. Those moments of respite from the shallow cruelty that was so common in the human world recharged me.

I do have to admit that your typical Elsie is not the greatest conversationalist and isn't much of a gourmet chef, but the bull in me was always looking forward to the cow life.

I went from herd to herd, never really settling anywhere, and I finally stole my way into the City of Lights a few years after the turn of the century. I settled into a cold run down room that turned out to be right in the middle of a community of starving artists. That's where I met Picasso.

Picasso was living in similar accommodations with Max, the poet. He worked at night and slept all day. I happened to pass by his room at about three in the morning and he saw my silhouette in the moonlight; at least that's what his excuse was for calling me to come up to his room. Thus began a friendship that lasted almost forty years.

I stood there in the light of his "studio," if you can call it that. The room was cold, the light was pale, and there was nothing but an easel, a canvas, and a palette of paint. He stared at me and asked me to pose one way, then another, then another.

"I think you'll do," he stated and then he turned back to the canvas he had been working on.

I wasn't sure what I could do for him, but I sat on the floor and waited to find out. He stood in front of a blank canvas for about a minute and then started sketching furiously. His hand darted up and down, back and forth, with quick lines and bold strokes until he stopped, smiled, and beckoned me to come. In the dim light I saw myself, a perfect image of me, but at the same time, something more. Sure, it looked like me, but the juxtaposition of human and bovine was delightfully accentuated. There was a combination of the fierce power of the bull contrasting with the intellect and artistry of the human. It was truly remarkable.

"You like it?" he asked, almost as an afterthought.

"It's amazing," I answered, trying to convey my enthusiasm and gratitude.

"It's trash," he added and he picked up the canvas and threw it on the fire. "I only keep those that are extraordinarily wonderful. The rest keep us warm. Come again tomorrow and I'll try to do better."

I went away confused, but that was Picasso. He saw things no one else could see and he wanted his art to be perfect. The night was cold, but I didn't mind. I still felt a sense of exhilaration, even if my image was doing nothing but warming the hands of a genius.

I wandered the streets as was my routine. Sometimes I stopped in at the cafés and clubs. Those that were open at such a late hour didn't care if I was human, bovine, serpentine, or fungus. The morals could only be described as loose, the food and drink was cheap, and the company stimulating. I became the great storyteller, spinning yarns about Crete,

Theseus, Africa, Egypt, and everything else. I always arrived after midnight; most of my audience was already drunk and/or stoned so I'm not sure anyone recalled even one of my tales. This actually worked to my advantage because I could tell the same story over and over and no one ever remembered.

But back to Picasso.

I went the next night and the night after and the night after. He would stand and paint while I sat back and listened. He spoke of his family, bull fighting, women, art, and the world. I told of him of my life, all the ups and downs, all the famous people I'd met, but mostly, I listened.

"The bull fight, now there is the classic struggle. The bull is powerful, virile, and full of passion. The matador clever, resourceful, and brave. And here you are, the perfect embodiment of each combined into one being. I will make you famous; I will fill the world with your image because it is my image, too.

"I see no reason to be the starving artist. A well-fed artist's work would be far superior. It is a myth that one must suffer for one's art. Let someone else suffer. As for me, I would do far better work with a full belly, a warm room, and a willing young lady.

"I'm done; let me show you."

He turned the easel around and there I was again, only now in a mixture of grays and blues. I was upside down, surrounded by ice and snow, obviously a representation of my frozen years. My face was a frozen scream, anguish stuck in time.

"I believe I shall keep this one, perhaps it will sell. It is far too perfect to be fodder for the fire," he announced. I was grateful.

"May I have it for my room?" I inquired. "I have nothing on my walls. It will remind of past times, better in some ways, but bitter in some ways, also."

He was silent for a minute.

"If I can't sell it in the next week, it is yours. But I need to eat and I think it will bring me a few francs. As I said, I prefer not to be a starving artist."

I stared at that painting for almost an hour. Besides myself, snow and ice, there were faint images of the burning bush and a crucifixion, both in the background, manifestations of the powerful dreams I'd had over and over during my thousand-year hibernation.

I wish I could say that those years in Paris were full of adventure or excitement. I suppose if I measured by modern day standards, Paris would be utterly boring. Daytime was for sleeping, nights were spent in cafés, or wandering the streets, or sitting in Picasso's studio. Those nights were the best.

Most of the time he painted, sometimes me, sometimes his current subject: still lifes, nudes of Fernande, landscapes, whatever piqued his interest. If he didn't feel like painting, I would try my hand, but unfortunately I had very little talent. Most of my attempts at portraits resulted in both eyes being on the same side of the face, curves ending up as squares, body parts grotesquely distorted. My attempt to copy his nude portrait of one young lady ended up like a caricature, her slightly prominent nose greatly exaggerated, plump lips far too big, curves that should have been square and squares that should have been curves. Her ample bosom took on monstrous proportion and her buttocks were more like two great beach balls.

"It's kindling," I declared as I prepared to throw it on the fire.

"Wait!" he exclaimed. "It only needs a bit of fine tuning."

He stood before the canvas and drew, painted, drew some more, and painted a bit more, his hands moving at lightning speed from one point to the next. When he finished, he stood aside to let me admire my work. Only it wasn't really my work anymore. All of my grotesque distortions were still there, only now they enhanced the image. The portrait was unmistakable. It was the perfect image of the model, but not. The round breasts were hers, but more angular, her nose and eyes jumped off the canvas, the angles were exaggerated, the curves accentuated. It was a masterpiece, an unprecedented interpretation of the female form.

And that is how I "invented" cubism.

Or, rather, how I inspired Pablo Picasso to do so.

31.

PICASSO EXPRESSED HIS VIEWS WITH great force and certainty.

On women:

"Oh, my dear Minotaur, the greatest gift God ever bestowed upon man is woman. Every man should have at least one woman in his life, and it is better to be generous towards the fairer sex. We give them our heart, our soul, our very life. And what do they return to us? Great pleasure, sustenance, life renewing itself, all of this and more. We let them look into the center of our soul and tell them: 'Please, take what you will, take all that I have to give.' A life devoid of the beauty that is woman is, indeed, a truly empty life."

I supposed my life had been more empty than full, but I really didn't feel that way. So I asked:

"What would you say about my long and seemingly endless life?"

"I would say that you are the most blessed being who ever walked on this planet."

"Why is that?"

"Because you are history. In that massive head is witness to extraordinary events. Things that are only in books, and we both know how such 'facts' can be distorted. Look at me; I paint what I see, what I feel. But I'm limited to my thoughts and imagination. You... you transcend mere imagination. You have experiences that I could only dream about. From your childhood to life among the cows, to your encounters with all the famous and infamous, you are history and a priceless treasure."

"I believe you were talking about women," I said, redirecting him back to the subject at hand.

"My paintings try to do justice to the perfection of the female form. Soft and curved, smooth skin, and a woman's face, such exquisite beauty. Not like a man. Women were made for the artist, to give us something beautiful and to keep us from starving."

On friendship:

"A man can never have too many friends. If one has friends then it is impossible to starve or be without shelter or clothes. True friends will always come through, even more than family. I have so little, my family gives me almost nothing, yet I have Max and Apollinaire, Breton, Jary, Gertrude Stein, even Matisse. I call all of them friend and I know I could count on each to come to my aid. I feel sorry for you, Minotaur. You have lived for so many years, yet you've never had a true friend. So many have deserted you in your times of greatest need. Nebuchadnezzar, Theseus, Vlad, even Jesus all abandoned you or turned on you. But I will never do such a thing. Plus, my art will make you great and famous."

I believed him at the time and he did make me famous, far more than mere myth. He wove me in and out of his work, including his great masterpiece, *Guernica*.

On war:

"War has to be the greatest waste of humanity ever. Why must someone always want what someone else possesses?

Why must innocent young men be forced to fight to settle someone else's differences? And why has war been with us for so many thousands of years? I wish I knew the answer to just one of these questions. And look at the weapons we have now. A large rock doesn't have much range nor can a club kill from afar. Swords and knives increase the killing potential, spears and arrows even more. But leave it to man to invent deadlier and deadlier weapons of destruction. Guns and bombs and airplanes now make it possible to kill someone across a continent. I just don't know, evil pops up and those who are supposed to be good try to force it down, and those who were good are just as evil. Is there an answer?"

Guernica was his answer to war and I was gratified to be included (I modeled the bull) in such a great masterpiece.

I lived in Paris for more than forty years. I lived through upheaval and the first Great War, content to spend my days in my small cold room, my nights divided between walking through the "City of Lights" or along the Seine, telling stories in late night cafés, or sitting with Picasso as he worked and talked. Other artists included my image in their work, but none could match Picasso. As he became more successful, he escaped that cold, dim room and moved to lighter, airier accommodations. I stayed behind, happy to have a place to lay my head. I had long outgrown any need for creature comforts. To his credit, Picasso did offer to find me a more comfortable room, but I politely declined.

Those years in Paris were what I would call calm, restful, and educational. Even though Montparnasse was the great bohemian center for artistic innovation, it was sedate compared to ancient Greece, Canaan, Rome, Transylvania, Luther's Germany, or even Victorian London. Besides the many hours I spent with the great painter, I met and conversed with many of the great minds of the day. It seems many of them frequented the same Montparnasse venues that I gravitated towards, always late at night. I wonder if you can picture me sporting a black beret, puffing on a thin French cigarette, conversing with Bergson, Sartre, Mounier, and so many others. They were all fascinated by my views on humanity, particularly on my unshakable belief in the underlying depravity of just about every man I had met.

Most of them disagreed which made for some very lively discourse, arguments that lasted until five or six in the morning. Several bottles of fine French wine and blocks of cheese accompanied the infamous French stubbornness. Such debates lived on through the Great War and were still gathering steam when World War II began. Although Picasso hated all wars, I knew he despised the Germans and found it difficult to hold back his feelings when they rolled into Paris. I did my best to avoid the occupiers' scrutiny, but they found me out. I was viewed as an imperfect, mutant oddball, certainly not in line with the German perception of acceptable humanity. Despite loud protests from the intelligentsia, I was arrested and shipped off in a cattle car (appropriate in my case, I guess) to the East, to be interred until "the time would be deemed proper for my release."

I disembarked in Poland at a camp called Auschwitz.

32.

PARIS IS THE CITY OF Lights; Auschwitz could only be called the camp of doom. I had been tied up and thrown into the car with a motley crew of the sick, injured, crippled, and degenerate. We shared only one thing: fear. Being the most bizarre among the bizarre, the others left me alone, bound, cold and unable to move. I was back in the frozen North, but with brutality and hatred added to the mix; I didn't think I'd survive this new and cruel Labyrinth. The train continued on through the day and night until it came to a sudden stop in the middle of the night. The doors were thrust open and silhouettes of angry guards appeared and ordered everyone out.

Being hogtied in a dark corner of the car, I was unable to comply and I actually thought I'd be forgotten. I figured I'd be cast out with the rest of the dead, but no such luck. One of the guards had been informed of my presence. He called for help as he cut the rope from my legs and in a very forceful way, told me to get up. I was stiff after the long ride and barely managed to get to my feet and walk down the plank, blinded by a spotlight that shined from the roof of the dark building ahead. I saw two tall smoke stacks atop two nondescript rectangular buildings. The air was filled with an unusual odor, a combination of burning meat and manure. It was a smell that never ceased and one that I soon equated with horrible death.

The lot of us was herded into a fenced-in area in front of the building on the right. The silhouette of a uniformed man stood on a low platform before us and began to scream in German.

"Welcome to Auschwitz, your new home. The Third Reich is your new benefactor. You will be housed here, fed, cared for until your home country is safe from our enemies. Before you are assigned to your barracks we will give you a shower, new clothes, and a hot meal. When the doors open please proceed into the shower room. Remove your clothes and wait for the water to be turned on. When you are finished you will be issued the necessary provisions."

The fear diminished after this speech. As promised, the doors opened and we were ushered into a huge, communal shower room where the men and women were separated. When they saw me they weren't sure where I should go, but one of the guards sent me with the women and children.

A little girl looked up at me and then clung tightly to her mother's leg.

"I know I must look very scary, little one," I said softly, "but, I am just as frightened."

She relaxed a fraction, but still held tightly to her mother's hand. Her mother took little notice of my unusual appearance, the fear and worry consuming her thoughts. Something as mundane as the Minotaur was not a concern.

Before long, we all stood huddled together, naked, waiting for the shower to commence. A whistle sounded and the shower heads began to spew forth. My eyes started to sting and my flesh began to feel like it was on fire. There was no water, only gas. After a few moments my companions began to slump to the ground, while I just stood there, the gas causing tears to run and my skin to crawl. It wasn't long before everyone was dead, but me. I wasn't sure if I should stay upright or slump over and pretend to be dead.

At that moment I realized that the stench I had noticed was from burning bodies and the smoke came from a huge oven. After the gas had receded and the doors opened I stood there defiantly. Guards rushed in, bound me, and carried me back to the anteroom. I was left in a corner while the dead were removed to the crematorium. Two guards started talking as they watched other inmates carry the dead away.

"What do we do with that freak?" one asked, I assumed referring to me.

"Throw it into the oven and see if it's also impervious to fire."

"I can't burn it alive. Maybe we should take it over to the camp doctor. You know do some tests or something, see what makes it tick."

"Maybe you're right. Better check with the commander."

I wasn't sure I wanted anyone to see what made me tick and I certainly had no idea why I was still alive. Then again, why should I survive being frozen for a thousand years or be able to live on almost no food in the Himalayas? Maybe it was finally time for some modern medical research. It wasn't long before the two guards returned, bound me once again, picked me up, threw me into a cart, and wheeled me across a snow-covered compound to the "medical" building.

I looked out over the camp as I crossed the open compound. There were rows and rows of wooden barracks and emaciated inmates all dressed in the same thin striped uniform. *Why do they need to gas these people when they're all on death's door as it is?* I pondered as I was deposited on a hard metal table.

"This is what you brought me? A bull? Just skewer the beast and don't waste my time," an annoyed voice said forcefully.

"Herr Doctor, the commandant has ordered that you investigate why it did not die in the gas chamber," one of the guards replied.

"Very well, but you need to stay with me to guard it and be ready to shoot if this beast becomes violent," the doctor answered.

I decided to speak up: "Violence is foreign to my nature, Doctor. You shall have nothing to fear from me, I assure you."

Both turned and stared at me. My fluent German and refined nature caught their attention. I was sure that they would realize that everything was just a big misunderstanding and put me on the next train back to Paris. What I got was a sharp rap between my eyes by the so-called doctor.

"This is obviously a mutant freak. Perhaps there *is* something to learn; it is worth some study. Strap him to this table, Corporal," the "doctor" commanded.

They tied me to a metal exam table, holding me down with heavy leather belts around my arms, legs, torso, neck, and head. Samples were taken of my blood, hair, saliva, stool, and every other bodily fluid they could obtain.

At least they didn't dissect me, was my only thought. They wheeled the exam table into a cold hospital ward and left me alone.

Maybe this will finally be the end. After so many centuries, after seeing the misery that was being dispensed in that camp, after all the brutality that humans seemed capable of, after so much suffering, death in any form would come as a relief. What I was given was a torment that was worse than death. They sent me back to the gas chamber.

I don't know what they were thinking or hoped to accomplish, but there I was, back in that familiar room, showerheads staring down at me, waiting to rain death. In short order, I was greeted by a new group of terrified, naked victims. All I could do was sit silently and cry for them, knowing their fate. They filed in and looked up anxiously at the pipes traversing the ceiling and waited. I wanted to shout, "Get out, don't come in," but all I did was sit silently as they perished.

I thought that would be the end, but I was left behind to face the next batch of innocent victims and the next and the next. Women and children, wave after wave and all I did was sit, cry, and sit.

I've got to do something, anything, was all that went through my head, over and over and over. *But you can't save them, they're all doomed.*

Yet maybe there was something I could do. Calm their fears, give them hope for something better. *Most of them are Jews; God is central to their lives. Tell them.*

And I did. My story, my experience, with Pharaoh, Moses, and Jesus. They would file in naked and vulnerable. Some would see me and gasp, step back in fright. Most barely noticed. Then I'd start my speech.

"It may seem to you at this moment that God has forsaken you, forsaken your people, forsaken the world. I am here to tell you that, even if you die, God's love for you still lives and you shall know it and experience it first-hand. I have lived through so many tribulations that tell me that God, your God, the God of Abraham, Isaac, and Jacob is alive. He is with us now and He will be with you always. He was with me, is with me, I have seen His work in person, seen His salvation. All I ask of you is to have faith. Even at this dark moment, when everything seems to be lost, you, every one of you, belongs to Him. If you believe this, have faith, there is nothing, absolutely nothing that the evil monsters that brought you here, who have stolen your dignity, stolen your very lives—there is nothing they can do to you. Because God is waiting for you and you shall be with Him, be it here or in Paradise."

Most of the time I only had time to say these few words before death rained down. I wasn't sure what I was trying to accomplish or if anyone listened or understood, until Greta.

She must have been about four years old and she had the brightest eyes I'd ever seen. She was huddling close to an elderly woman, her grandmother I presumed, as I spoke, but as I made my little speech she came close to me. By the time I finished she was sitting right by my foot and with the final word she jumped up and grabbed me around the leg. All I could do was embrace her and she whispered her name in my ear, "Greta," then it started. The gas poured out and still she clung to my leg. She coughed and gasped for air, but she held tightly to my leg. Finally, she went limp and all that remained were her arms wrapped around my leg. I stood there, an impotent prophet offering only empty words. Greta was gone. I wept and wept, the image of her bright eyes burned into my brain. I had to stop, give up the game, pray that no more Gretas were sentenced to grisly death. But others did come and come and come. There was no end to my misery. After all, could anyone watch such a parade of death day after day and just go on, pretending all was right with the world? I would give my little speech and watch them die and then the next crew would come; I'd give my speech, a little less enthusiastically and then watch them die. Every once in a while there was a real shower and I'd breathe a sigh of relief; hope would well up inside and I'd think, *It's finally over*. But death would begin anew.

It was like living in your modern movie *Groundhog Day*, only with a different cast each day. And like Bill Murray in that picture show, I sank deeper and deeper into a state of despair. Thousands upon thousands marched through that place and almost none walked out.

I finally gave up on trying to offer any solace and returned to the isolation of the Labyrinth, the image of little Greta clinging to my leg burned into my brain. The doomed marched in and all I could do was crouch in the corner. Other prisoners would come and clean up the dead, while I stayed hunched over in my corner. I was left in complete solitude, refusing to move. I longed for only one thing: to be free. Free from the suffering; free from watching little children gasp and choke and fall to the floor dead; free from watching mothers clutch their babies to their breast, trying to shield them from the inevitable; free from the smell of death and the constant stench of burning bodies.

I wept silent tears, never ate, never drank, and waited for my own demise. Finally, the tables turned. Those sentenced to die came to me to offer *their* words of comfort. First it was an old lady, nearly blind I suspect, who heard my faint cries, her ears sharpened by her years in darkness.

"Have faith, kind sir, even when there is nothing but misery and pain, God remains. He is here with us, with you, and He will deliver, if not here, then in the next life. Now stand tall and have faith."

Her words had been my words, only now they carried so much more meaning and the power of true faith. After her, more came, the old and infirm, children, mothers, the crippled, and the lame. They would come up to me, some just offering a light touch, others an embrace, and many more, a prayer. But I could not look at them, could not face another Greta. On and on, day after day, weeks and months and years my life continued to be filled with nothing but the stench of death. Finally, I looked upward and asked, aloud: "Why?"

I didn't expect an answer from a God that had long ago forsaken this world, but the death march stopped. For whatever reason, they stopped coming. I left that room and watched as the Germans tore it down, vain efforts to hide their evil deeds. Soon the Russians came and freed those that remained.

I wasn't able to speak Russian, but I surmised what the soldiers were thinking when they found me, a shell of my usual self, curled up on a bare mat in one of the barracks. They stood and stared, shaking their collective heads in unison. When they opened the gate I simply walked away. I'm sure they thought I was the product of an evil medical experiment. And they were correct; I was the product of a sadistic psychological experiment that left me bitter and even more convinced of the complete inhumanity of mankind.

33.

I WALKED AWAY FROM AUSCHWITZ, headed out to find a new life, something as far away from "normal" people as possible. I planned to go back to the bovine life for a while, perhaps forever. Although I usually got the cold udder from the Elsies, I'd never seen a cow murder, cheat, steal, or anything else that could be considered a violation of the basic truths of morality.

I walked along the roads and shook my head at the destruction of war. Bombed-out buildings, decimated forests, and not a herd of cows to be found. I presume they had also become casualties of war. I kept walking, out of Poland, through Czechoslovakia and Hungary, eventually finding my way back to Romania. It had changed tremendously since I'd last visited; a lot can happen in six hundred years.

I eventually found a farm that still had cattle and I spent a few months hidden among the Elsies and a few less-than-friendly bulls. The Elsies laughed at me and didn't give me much regard. It was after I'd once again resigned myself to living a life on the fringe of bovine society that things took a change and for once, for the better.

THE CIRCUS CAME TO TOWN

I don't know why I had never found one before. But this Greek troupe of acrobats, clowns, and sideshow attractions set up shop in the middle of my cow pasture. A big tent went up and I just watched them put their stage together, fascinated from the moment they arrived until the time the final stake was driven into the ground. More than anything, I was enamored of the "freaks," that is, the sideshow performers.

They had banded together: the dwarf couple, the tall man, the wolf girl, the goat man, the fat lady, and the strong man. They sat together outside one of the smaller tents, smoking cigarettes, drinking, laughing—in short, having a grand time. Their mood struck me as one of camaraderie, outcasts thrown together, sharing the joys and sorrows of being different. I belonged with them.

Why not? You're more different than any of them, I thought. I could simply saunter out and take a seat next to the wolf girl. *But what if they laugh at me, or drive me away? Can I take such rejection by people who are just as different as I am?*

Then, as I watched, the male dwarf kicked the goat man and the dwarf lady began to beat on her husband's back. It was almost comical until the goat man pulled out a knife with every intention of using it. I couldn't stand by and watch. I stood up and yelled in my ancient Greek dialect: "Stop, put down the knife!"

I don't know if it was my unusual appearance or my language, but the fighting ceased immediately and they each turned and stared at the bizarre creature that stood before them. The goat man dropped his knife to the ground as I walked towards them.

"Violence never solved any differences, my good people," I admonished. "A cordial discussion and vetting of all the facts is the best way to resolve any dispute."

"Talk about a freak," one dwarf whispered to the other.

The strong man took a few steps back as I approached, while the fat lady moved in front of the tall man. Only the wolf girl didn't move; she had a smile on her face.

"Allow me to introduce myself," I said casually. "I'm the Minotaur, well known of Greek mythology. Quintus is my name, but most people just call me Minotaur. I couldn't help but notice your circus, especially since you put it up in the middle of my pasture. When I saw the lot of you I couldn't help but think that you are a group of misfits not unlike myself and perhaps I could join your ragamuffin band."

At first, the goat man eyed me suspiciously, but then he overcame his fear and walked right up and pulled on my horns.

"I assure you, I am quite real. You probably believe the stories of my demise at the hand of that drunken fool, Theseus, but, as you can plainly surmise, those reports are greatly in error. I've been wandering around ever since. I never considered joining a circus, but it truly makes the most perfect sense," I observed.

"Well, you'll fit right in with the rest of us freaks, Minotaur," the fat lady stated in a high squeaky voice. "Let me introduce you. I'm Lavinia, the fat lady. These two short people are Genaro and his sister, Jin. The tall man is Landrew and the cowering strong man is Atlas. Jin's husband is the goat man, Pan. And this shy creature is Biz, the wolf girl."

"I'm very pleased to meet all of you," I said, "especially you, beautiful young lady."

I took Biz's hand and kissed as best as I could; she turned her head and giggled shyly.

"I would like to meet the leader of this circus and perhaps offer my services as an addition to the fine troupe of performers that is already assembled. Would you show me the way, Biz?" I asked gently. I offered my fingers which she accepted in her hair-covered hand and led me away to the ring leader's quarters.

The "Chief," as he was affectionately called, was a dark-skinned man, about forty, pudgy, with thick black hair and a big smile. When he saw me he nearly fell off his stool. When he regained his composure, he stood and enthusiastically shook my hand.

"This is Minotaur," Biz said softly. "He would like to join our circus."

"Sir," I added, "I believe I would be a great asset to your unique band of performers. As I'm sure you have surmised I am a rather unusual type. I am the original Minotaur of story and song. The rumors of my demise were greatly exaggerated and now I come to you from the ravages of war humbly requesting to be a part of your highly-esteemed circus."

"Quiet, quiet," he mumbled. "Turn around, lift up your arms. Smile. You're for real, that's for sure. You're hired. You start tonight. We don't have time to put together another platform for you so I think you should just go with Biz. We'll display the two of you together."

I bowed and shook his hand while Biz just smiled. During our brief acquaintance she seemed to have become enamored of me. I have to say that the feeling was mutual. To this day I have no idea why we connected the way we did.

Her appearance was different from every other person I had met in my long life. Hair covered her everywhere and was very thick on the top of her head, styled and curled, creating a very striking look. She had large brown eyes and a petite nose. Her thick red lips were not hairy and despite the fur that covered her, she had a beautiful body by human standards; all the right curves in right proportion. I'm not sure if it was her unique beauty which first caught my attention or her shyness.

That she was shy did not surprise me in the least. Years of being pointed at, laughed at, taunted to the point of tears would make even the strongest individual reticent to open up to another person. But she saw in me a soul mate, someone who had suffered as she had, and I have to say, I had similar feelings.

As we left the Chief's office she started to talk and talk and talk.

"I'm so happy that you're going to be with me in your first show. I think we'll make a great team. 'The Wolf and the Bull singing and dancing their way into your hearts.' Or, 'Minotaur and Wolf Woman, terrors of the freak show world.' What do you think?"

"I think you should slow down..." I started to say, but she jumped right in again.

"No, you've come here as the answer to so many prayers and I'm so afraid I'll lose you. I never knew that there could be somebody as different as I am and then *you* walk into my life. It's simply amazing. Where were you before you came here? Where did you hide during the war? We hid in a barn. Lavinia said that if the Nazis found us they'd ship us away and most likely kill us. We were so happy when the war finally ended. I hated being cooped up in that barn, barely enough food, risking our lives to go out and take a bath in the stream, always at night so that we wouldn't be seen. So tell me, where were you during the war?"

I gave a brief sigh and closed my eyes. "I began the war in Paris, but that didn't last. When the Germans marched into that city they found me and sent me away." She stopped talking after that and we walked on in silence.

"Here is my tent. This is where we'll perform the shows. Usually, I start the show crouched on all fours like a real wolf. They keep the room dark and I make growling and howling noises. AA... OOOOO! AA... OOOOO!" She howled twice. "Pretty good, huh?" she asked.

"Just wonderful," I remarked, happy that the subject had turned away from the war.

"Anyway, after the howling shtick, the room gets lighter and I put my arms on this table and pull myself up. Then I start to talk, usually something sort of silly and trite, like,

212 | Minotaur Revisited

'You've heard of the wolf man and werewolves, but have you ever heard of the wolf woman?' And I'll bare my teeth. My only props are these fake fangs and they always get some *oohs* and *ahs* and the occasional scream. Then the lights come on completely and I stand straight up and howl again, 'AA... OOOOO!' Well, by this howl the room is usually pandemonium and people are standing up and fainting and running out. And then the big finish: I break through the fence that is supposed to keep me separated from the audience. Most of the audience scatters by this point, but if anyone remains I dart towards them. That's when my assistants run out and harness me. Pretty good, don't you think?"

"Amazing," I replied. "Where will I fit in?"

"We'll have to come up with something new. We've got a couple of hours before the first show. Let's have lunch and maybe the others can help us come up with some ideas."

Lunch consisted of brown bread, Swiss cheese, and wine. After the deprivation and self-imposed starvation of Auschwitz, the repast was a gourmet delight. My new companions seemed more than happy to allow me seconds and thirds, all except for Lavinia, who scowled at my third helping.

"Perhaps a song and dance together?" Jin suggested.

"Maybe the two of you should fight," Pan added.

"Jump out at the audience."

"Put on a little show."

None of the suggestions seemed to catch the proper spirit of two freakish misfits confronting a world that had offered nothing but torment.

"Biz, just do your regular thing and I'll come up with something," I finally said.

"OK, but the Chief'll be expecting something special," she replied.

I wasn't sure what I was going to do and I decided that when the time came I'd improvise. Here's what I did:

Biz did her usual routine, very convincingly I must add, and I could tell she had more than her usual enthusiasm. As the big finished approached, the part where she breaks out into the audience only to be restrained by the circus personnel, I jumped out from behind the curtain and charged into the already terrified crowd. Not only did I jump out at them, I followed them out of the tent. Now not only was our audience in a panic, but the entire circus began to run for cover from the fierce Minotaur. I didn't go very far and returned to our tent. The Chief was waiting and he did not look pleased.

"Thought you were pretty clever out there today, eh, Minotaur? Scare everyone, give them a great show!" he shouted, his voice rising with each word, the big vein on his forehead turning purple and popping out until I thought it would burst.

"I think I accomplished the desired effect," I answered, nonchalantly.

"THE DESIRED EFFECT! THE DESIRED EFFECT!" he shouted. "You almost got everyone killed. I ought to kick the both of you out. Come up with something different for the evening show."

"Nobody appreciates art," I observed, shaking my head, while trying to hide the smile on my face.

Biz sat next to me and took my hand. "We'll have to do something a bit tamer tonight," she said.

We thought long and hard about what to do. Nobody had any good ideas, but fate was in our favor. As we fretted about the evening performance, a huge crowd gathered. The line stretched all the way to the edge of the field until our tent was overflowing. The Chief came by and, to no one's surprise, instructed us to do the show exactly as we had done it before. So we did, again and again and again. People came from villages ten, twenty, even a hundred miles away to see the wolf girl and the fierce Minotaur.

I was happier than I'd been in many years. The horror of the Holocaust began to fade, replaced by the light Biz brought into my life. We became inseparable. I, of course, told her my story; all my stories from Theseus to Auschwitz. She listened with her head against my massive bovine shoulder and closed her eyes as I talked about Moses or Jesus or Vlad. She asked to hear the story of my imprisonment in the cave over and over. She would glance upward, touch *the* spot on my head, and then wrap her arms around me and smile.

The circus travelled throughout Eastern Europe, going from Romania, to Yugoslavia, to Czechoslovakia, to Poland and then back, always stopping in small towns and villages. Everywhere we went the people lined up to see the fierce beasts: The Wolf Girl and The Minotaur. We varied the show; sometimes I would start out on the stage while she would be the one hidden until the end, and sometimes we sang silly songs as the light grew brighter and our dispositions grew meaner until we'd break out into the audience. The Chief didn't care what we did as long as people felt like they were entertained and no one was hurt. For me, the show was mostly a great nuisance; get it over with so that I could get back to the business of Biz.

There was one incident that occurred in Poland which I think had great significance apart from my budding romance. We were somewhere in central Poland, putting on our show as usual, when I noticed a boy that kept hanging around the circus. I saw him standing on the outskirts of the field as we prepared, then I watched him wander between the tents, then I saw him in the audience at our show. After each performance, and I think he must have seen the show at least ten times, he would hang around to catch a glimpse of me and Biz. Well, on the fifth day I saw him in the usual place after the show and I went up to him.

"You must like the show, young man. I've seen you here at every performance," I observed.

At first he seemed frightened. He couldn't have been more than seven years old with beautiful eyes and an inquisitive look on his face.

"How did you get to be the way you are?" he asked boldly.

"You mean so big and handsome? Or, that I look like a bull?" I replied.

"I mean, how is it that you look so different and how can you stand looking the way you do?"

"I've been around for a lot of years. If people don't like me the way I am, well, that's their problem."

He thought about this for a few moments.

"I sometimes feel different," he finally said. "I know that I don't look different, but I think I see things differently." He looked around, first over one shoulder, then the other, as if someone was spying on him. "Ever since the war ended and my father died, I've had feelings like this. We have so little and the people are so frightened all the time; first the Germans and now the Russians. Did you fight in the war? I bet the Germans would have been really scared of you."

I closed my eyes briefly as I remembered my war days. "I was in a camp during the war," I finally answered.

"My father was in a camp. He said he was cold and hungry all the time. He died only two months after he came home."

"I'm sorry," was all I could say.

"I didn't really know him. I was born while he was in the camp and he was always sick after he came home and then he died. Momma cried a lot at first." He was silent for a few moments and then he remarked, "I think it would be fun to be in the circus, and then I wouldn't have to worry about Momma or people being hurt or dying. I could just perform, make people happy all the time."

"It's not fun and games all the time, you know. You can never be settled and there's work to do besides the performing. It is gratifying to see the joy we bring to the people who watch us, but that's just for a moment. There is so much more than a few brief smiles from a circus. I've lived a lot of years and I've seen what evil men can do. It's those individuals who stand up to this evil that bring true happiness, to themselves and everyone they touch. A circus may be fun, but a boy like you should be in search of something more."

He mulled my words over and over in his head as he stared at his feet. Then looked me right in the eye.

"For a fierce monster, you know a lot about different things. Maybe the circus isn't right for me. I'm going to do something that helps all the people. I'm going to be one of those people that stand up to evil. Just watch me." He looked up at the sun. "It's late. I need to go. Thanks, Mr. Minotaur."

As he ran away I called out to him, "What's your name young man?"

He turned as he ran and shouted, "Lech... my name is Lech."

I don't know if he was the same Lech that led Poland's uprising against communism, but I wouldn't be surprised.

Biz and I continued to develop our show adding new, frightening, and mysterious touches. Sometimes one of us would sit in the middle of the audience, disguised; instead of bounding into the audience from offstage, we'd now be right in the middle. People scattered in every direction. We added props that created an eerie nighttime-in-the-cemetery effect, enhanced by creepy ghoulish sounds. We recruited other performers to add even more scary visuals. We soon had a full-scale haunted house with Biz and me as its stars. The Chief was thrilled with the growing revenue so he gave us free reign to develop our craft.

Off-stage Biz and I remained inseparable. One day after the show we were relaxing in my tent when I decided it was time to pop the question.

"Biz, I've never been as happy as I've been these last months. You have made me complete. Years and years of misery have been washed away and I'm finally free of the Labyrinth," I said, my voice wavering. "Are you happy, too?"

"Oh, Quint, you know I am. No one... never in my life has anyone been so good to me. We really are meant for each other. We should be married," she stated, taking the words right off the tip of my tongue.

I looked at her in amazement and coolly nodded my approval. I then smiled as best as I could and then we gave each other a big hug and kiss before heading out to tell all the cast and crew.

34.

AND SO WE WERE MARRIED. Biz was not one for long engagements and after thousands of years I saw no reason to procrastinate. We rounded up a priest, picked a bouquet of flowers, bought a couple of cheap rings, and got hitched. There was a big party and we convinced the Chief to let us take a few days off for a honeymoon, and that was that.

I loved her more than anything and I guess my feelings overshadowed some of the practical concerns that popped into my mind later.

First there was the age difference. I was over three thousand years old and she was nineteen. This was only a theoretical problem. Physiologically, I was a young, robust (well healthy, anyway) bull and I intended to remain that way. She certainly was at the peak of her youthful beauty. She had no worries, therefore I dismissed mine.

Second was the issue of aging. I had been born with an unnatural tendency towards immortality, something she definitely lacked. What would happen as she aged and I remained in the prime of life? I secretly hoped that the exchange of bodily fluids inherent in the marriage commitment would grant her long life as the drinking of my blood had done for that scoundrel, Vlad.

Third was the potential problem of children. Would we have any? What would they be like? Would they be bovine? Hairy? Normal Humans? Boys? Girls? I wouldn't want any offspring to have to endure suffering like us, but I also knew that a child would be a blessing.

At first, I kept these questions bottled up inside, but Biz could tell something was upsetting me. When I shared my concerns she only smiled.

"Why let such trivial things interfere with our happiness?" she asked with a twinkle in her eye. "We have each other now and even if it's only for one hour, it would be enough for a lifetime."

She wrapped her arms around my thick neck and kissed me, and I knew she was right. My worries melted away in her arms and we went on, sharing our wonderful life together.

We were ecstatically happy for years. Circus life gave us the usual ups and downs common to any marriage and we spent every moment together: eating, sleeping, performing, romancing, practicing new routines. Biz and I sometimes broke up the monotony of the show by stopping in the middle of the scariest parts to sing a silly duet together, or dance a tango, or even recite a bit of poetry. It was all fun and the ever-growing crowds ate it up. We toured throughout Eastern Europe, visiting smaller towns, avoiding the larger cities and the glowering eyes of Communism.

The circus provided the opportunity for me to visit many of my old homes and give Biz a glimpse into my past. We visited Crete and walked on the ground which had been the Labyrinth; we visited Athens, Egypt, Germany, and so many other places.

We made a stop in Italy where I spied Picasso in the audience. I suppose he couldn't resist seeing his old friend in a new light. He looked so much older and defeated, as if life was weighing him down. It was now the early sixties and he had reached amazing commercial success, but to my eye, he had lost the creative spark. The remarkable talent that had taken the amateurish scrawling of an untalented freak and turned it into the greatest artistic phenomenon of the century, talent which had produced one of the greatest pieces of antiwar art ever, was beaten down by personal tragedy and age. Very sad. After the show I waited for him to visit backstage, but he didn't come. Biz and I went to his villa, but security at the entrance would not even announce us. I left with a touch of remorse over my lost friend.

We stopped in Wittenberg and I showed Biz where forty-five of Brother Martin's theses flew away on the wind.

We almost went to Auschwitz. We rode towards that camp of horror, but as we approached the entrance, tears welled up in my eyes and we had to turn around; the pain was too great.

And we performed, selling out everywhere we went. Biz started composing her own silly songs which we sang together after the scary part of the show was finished. I have to say those were the happiest years of my life, perhaps the only truly happy time I'd ever experienced. I thought we would go on forever. She seemed to be forever young, just like me, but then she found the lump.

She showed it to me one night; just a small lump on her side. She said it had been the size of a pea when she'd first noticed it a few weeks before, but now it was lima bean size. The hair over it grew a shade darker than the rest of her "fur," and it didn't hurt; rather it just rolled around under her skin. The lump stopped growing for a while and we didn't think any more of it until the hair covering it fell out. Beneath had been hidden some nasty looking black skin. We were in Romania at that time and we took her to the local physician, Dr. Krokau.

"Very unusual. Very unusual, indeed," he said solemnly. "You must see this man in Budapest, an excellent Dermatologist, Dr. Meinsger. Here is his number and a letter of introduction."

We put the show on hold and left immediately.

Dr. Meinsger was waiting for us when we arrived. He made no comment at first, not about me, not about Biz, just poked and scraped and poked some more. He ran his hand over every inch of her body. From head to toe, listened with his stethoscope, looked in her eyes and ears and mouth. He took out a magnifying glass and studied the black spot. Finally, he produced a little cylinder, put some cream on the spot, and took out a piece of the nasty lump.

"What is it, Herr Doctor?" I started to ask, but he shook his head and continued his poking and prodding.

"You will come back in two days and I will have the answer," he finally said.

So we left. We spent the next two days seeing the sites in Budapest, shopping at some of the quaint little shops we discovered and mostly, silently worrying. The second night Biz finally broke down.

"Quint," she began as her hair became damp with tears, "I've never been so frightened. You know what Dr. Meinsger is going to say, we both do. Look at the lump now." She held her arm up and she showed me the lump which had tripled in size. "And feel right here."

She lifted her arm and I felt underneath, finding a lump the size of a tennis ball. I stared into her tear-filled eyes that identically matched my own. We didn't say another word that night, just held each other until we passed into fitful sleep. We were both up before the sun, preparing for the worst. At ten a.m. we were sitting in Dr. Meinsger's office.

"Melanoma," he stated, "very unusual in someone with your underlying condition, but I'm afraid it is at an advanced stage. There isn't any good treatment, although there is experimental work going on all the time. I think you should go to America, see the doctors at the Mayo Clinic. If anyplace has anything to offer, it's there."

We didn't waste any time in setting off for the United States, not giving a second thought to our unusual appearance. We flew first class and ignored the "ooh's" and "ah's" and the complaints about my horns. None of that mattered; I, for one, was oblivious to everything but Biz. She maintained an upbeat attitude, but she was terrified. Still, she seemed a bit more excited about visiting the States than I was. Cowboys and wild frontiers were not my style so I was taken by surprise when we landed in New York City and the Wild West was nowhere to be seen, only skyscrapers and taxicabs.

We spent the night at The Plaza Hotel, occupying a fine suite on the tenth floor. We drew a bit of attention at first with our eastern European accents and unusual clothing. We took advantage of the diversity New York offered and dined out at Sukaya, a wonderful Japanese restaurant. This was the first time we'd tried sushi and we met the raw fish with a bit of trepidation. Biz loved it; I could take it or leave it. We walked around Central Park, visited the United Nations, and then said goodbye to the Big Apple, boarding the jet for Minnesota, full of hope.

We spent an uneventful night at the hotel. Biz mostly talked about the future.

"I like this country, everything is so new and so open," she remarked. "I'd like to settle here. I'm ready to retire from circus life. Maybe we can adopt some children."

"We can certainly look into it," I responded, doing my best to play along with her upbeat banter while we both attempted to ignore the hurdles we faced ahead.

"The people talk funny here," I added. "I can barely understand them. The countryside around this city reminds me of Switzerland without the mountains. Maybe Minnesota would be a nice place to retire to."

At that moment she looked up at me and tears filled her eyes. "Do... do you think we'll get to retire together?" she sobbed as tears rolled down her cheeks.

I sat next to her, picked her up, and held her tightly to my chest. "Of course we will, my little Biz, we'll always be together."

I held her that way silently until she fell asleep and I gently tucked her into bed before climbing in beside her. But I couldn't sleep. I stared at the ceiling hoping against hope for a sign that would tell me everything was going to be OK.

Biz was in much better spirits the next morning as we drove up to the imposing brick building with the red and white sign announcing our arrival to the world famous "Mayo Clinic."

We found room 123, went through the necessary registration, and sat down to wait. After what seemed an eternity we were ushered into Dr. Stimson's office, where he was waiting behind a huge mahogany desk. His credentials stared down at us from the walls, but his face beamed a smile that softly conveyed the message: "I know you're scared, but you can trust me to do everything that my knowledge and skill allow to ease your pain and suffering."

He took Biz into the exam room while I waited in his office. I studied his diplomas, got up and walked back and forth, and then looked out the window. I read and reread every certificate on the wall, noting that he graduated from the University of Minnesota Medical School in 1950, finished his Internal Medicine residency in 1953, did additional training in Oncology, and was Board Certified in Internal Medicine. Finally, I sat back down and closed my eyes, only to bounce back up and pace the floor until the door finally opened. Biz returned alone.

"How did it go?" I asked as I put my arms around her waist. "Did he tell you anything?"

"He didn't say much, really. He did the usual poking and prodding and felt all around. They took some blood and did some X-Rays. Dr. Stimson said to wait here. He was going to look at the X-Rays. I don't know what to think. He looked so serious; I wish he'd smiled at least once during the exam."

"It'll be OK. I trust this doctor. He's got very kind eyes. He looks like Jesus. It would be nice if he could perform miracles."

At that moment the door opened and Dr. Stimson came in. He sat in his big leather chair and we took our spots across from him.

"Your Hungarian doctor was right, I'm sorry to say. You have melanoma, a type of skin cancer that grows very aggressively. I'm sorry to say that your X-Rays revealed that the cancer has spread to your bones and probably to your liver. There is not any effective treatment for disease like yours. There are some experimental tests being done on new types of therapy, but they are in very early stages and I don't think they will help you. I'm sorry."

We both sat speechless, completely dumbfounded by the bluntness and finality of his words. He sat motionless across the desk from us, patiently waiting for our response. My throat filled with anger and I felt like reaching out and grabbing him—or someone—by the throat, but Biz stopped me as she spoke.

"Thank you, Dr. Stimson. You've been more than kind and I appreciate your forthright diagnosis. Now if you'll excuse me, I have arrangements to make."

Biz's calm demeanor sucked the anger out of me. We stood up, shook Dr. Stimson's hand, and prepared to leave.

"Biz," the doctor said as we were walking out the door. "If you should start to suffer, feel pain... If you need any help, please call me day or night, anytime."

"Thank you, Doctor. I shall keep that in mind, but I don't think I will suffer. Quint is all the comfort I will need." And we left.

35.

WE HAD NO IDEA HOW much time we had left, but we made the best of a difficult situation. At first we planned to buy a car and drive across the country, see the sites, meet the people, and savor our last days together. There was one minor problem with this plan; neither one of us knew how to drive. The train seemed like a good alternative so we purchased two unlimited travel tickets, reserved their finest Pullman car, and headed out to see the US of A.

Our last few weeks together were like a movie montage of historical sites. With late nights out dining and dancing, attending concerts and shows, spending leisurely days boating on pristine lakes and finally, quiet moments in the mountains of Colorado. We went from town to city on every train imaginable, met the people, and lived ten lifetimes in two months.

It was those last serene, intimate, unforgettable days away from civilization which I carry buried deep in my heart and soul. We found a house on a secluded lake with the next closest dwelling at least five miles away. It was late spring and the weather was perfect. It was as if God wanted our last moments together to be a special gift.

We started each day with an early morning walk through the woods and along the lake. She loved that time of day, especially when the sun was out, but it was still cool. She would bundle herself up in a sweater and wrap her arm around mine. After centuries of being exposed to every imaginable confluence of weather, I was pretty much immune to cold or heat or any extreme in-between.

That last morning she talked about what she thought was waiting for her in the afterlife. I need to add at this point that over the years she had listened to all my stories over and over, never tiring of hearing about Alena, Mata, Moses, Brother Martin, and all the rest. Mostly she liked to hear about Jesus, about the cave, about His touch. Particularly in these last few months, she took great comfort from this story, far more than I ever did.

"I can't wait to meet Him," she would say. "All the pain of this world, all the suffering will be gone and I bet they'll give me the most perfect body. No more cancer, beautiful, smooth skin, and such peace. Yes, it will be wonderful."

"You're already the most beautiful and perfect person in the world," I replied. "The first time I saw you I fell in love and it's just been more and more ever since."

"Quint, you've been the shining star for me in this world. If I hadn't found you, I would've left this world behind long ago. Who knows where I'd be now; someplace bad, no doubt. You brought joy and laughter and beauty into my life, so many things I'd never known. I never told you this, I never told anyone, but that very week you showed up at the circus, I'd already decided was going to be my last. I was going to go out in grand style. I had a gun and when all those horrid spectators were at the height of their gawking I was going to do it. I was going to go into my act, but at the last moment, I was going to turn from the audience and put that gun in my mouth and blow my brains out—all over my "fans." That would have been quite a show to remember. You saved me; you gave me all these wonderful years. I love you so much. The only thing I regret about leaving this world is leaving you."

Tears filled my eyes as I grabbed her and held her as tight as I could.

"You've saved me in so many ways, dear Quint," she whispered. She closed her eyes and we held each other silently for what seemed like hours.

"I'm feeling a little tired," she said after a while. "Maybe we can lie down?"

I carried her to the bedroom and laid her on the bed, propped a pillow under her head, and then went into the kitchen to get some water. When I returned she was gone, so peaceful, so serene, with a smile on her face. I picked her up and held her to my chest. I let out a roar and then tears filled my eyes. I held her that way until night fell.

That evening, I buried her by the lake she loved so much. I marked her grave with a large dark-gray boulder surrounded by a circle of rocks and scratched into the stone, "BIZ, Forever My Love."

I stayed at the lake for a few weeks until I couldn't take it anymore. Every ripple of waves on the lake, every buzz from the insects, every rustle of the wind, every sight, sound, and smell cried out BIZ. I knew I had to go. I locked the door, put the key under the mat, and left. I headed west to San Francisco. The year was 1967.

I thought it would be another Montparnasse, the bohemian creative hotspot of Paris. I suppose I was trying to relive those glorious days and find the heir to Picasso; one who would appreciate my superb modeling skills. Haight-Ashbury, however, was not Montparnasse.

Instead of finding the bohemian and cerebral world that had been Montparnasse, I found a society filled with unkempt, slovenly, pseudointellectual dropouts whose creative skills were limited to shallow poetry set to what they called music. Bach it was not. Of course, this is my perspective looking backwards. At the time I was full of hope; hope in the idealism of youthful inspiration and vision.

I found a small apartment only a few blocks from the popular clubs and coffee houses. I wasn't very surprised that no one seemed shocked by my unusual appearance. Bizarre costumes ruled the day and I, more or less, fit right in. Downstairs and a few doors over was the Beat Coffee Shoppe. I suppose the British spelling added a bit of class. This is where I spent much of my time, slowly sipping creamy coffee, dining on homemade pastries, telling my tale, and offering counsel to anyone that cared to listen. Over three thousand years of hobnobbing with great historical icons gave me, I believed, some insight into the human (and bovine) condition. Cows, being less complex than people, made for very dull conversation, however, so I restricted my commentary to humanity.

I became known as the "Ancient Greek Guru," and they all came to me. There was John, Denny, Michelle, Cass, Jerry, Bob, another John, Lou, Roger (aka John), Barry, and so many others. I never learned any of their last names and I never bothered to learn what they did with my advice. All I know is they usually seemed to be in a faraway place—mentally, that is—and they dressed in a most untidy fashion.

They also asked silly, trite questions. I felt like I was back in my cave in the Himalayas, being approached by shallow people who saw great meaning in drivel. Here are some of the questions I was asked:

"Do you think LSD expands the mind into other dimensions?"

No, it just fries your brain into tapioca so that the user becomes no better than a bowl of green Jell-O.

"Do you believe that we are all entitled to free, unfettered sex?"

There's no such thing as free love or sex. Everything worth having comes with a price.

"The Bible says, 'There is a season for everything.' When is the season for peace going to come?"

The Book of Ecclesiastes carries a great deal of wisdom, but its central theme is the importance of God above everything else. Everything "under the sun" is mere vanity.

"Should I eat only wheat bread?"

I guess this questioner was a visionary; wheat is better than white I suppose. Actually, I'm not a nutritionist. To me bread is bread.

Then there were the artists, but Picasso they were not. I don't know why they had this compulsion to show me their faux impressionistic "modern" art. A white canvas with two black dots in the middle called "Angst," a series of red and black blotches titled "Desire in the Desert," finger painting stick-trees in purple and calling it "Muse," and I could go on and on.

I have nothing against the abstract, but there should be some sort of substance, a sense of medium and style, not random shapes and colors devoid of even the slightest artistic sense. Most of the time I would sit in my straight-backed wooden chair and nod my head in a cryptic sort of way, which allowed the would-be artist to invent an interpretation that fit their needs. It was all I could do to keep from vomiting at the nonsensical junk they called "art."

After the summer, I reached the limits of my patience and started seeking something new. I left Haight-Ashbury with the first cold rain of the fall; I just got up one day and started walking, south I think. I walked from here to there, without any purpose, perhaps in an attempt to return to the Labyrinth. I walked along the highway, startling cars as they whizzed by. I slept on beaches and in woods, avoiding humans, cows, everyone and everything. I had no idea what I wanted; all I knew was that I was tired. In retrospect I was still grieving over Biz's untimely death.

The most memorable part of these aimless wanderings was the dreams.

36.

THEY WERE UNLIKE THE DREAMS of my frozen years, yet in some ways were similar. One dream recurred over and over, always putting me back in the Labyrinth, the *real* Labyrinth of Crete. I'd be tending a vineyard or a grove of olive trees, minding my own business, content to live the solitary life, when one of my many acquaintances would appear.

Theseus, Alena, Mata, Martin, John, Vlad, Moses, and all the others, except Jesus, appeared at one time or another. As soon as that night's participant arrived, a large gold door would materialize in the middle of the Labyrinth. Joyful noise, like that of a huge party, could be heard on the other side of that door. My visitor would always stop and look at me, never uttering a word. Whoever it was would then stare at the door; sometimes stopping to think, sometimes gently knocking, sometimes turning the golden knob to see if it would open.

And the result was always different. Sometimes the door opened by itself, a bright light shined through, and my visitor would pass through, *always* begging me to accompany them (which I politely declined). Other times the visitor had to turn the knob and, with some difficulty, pull the door open. They would have to be quick to pass through, because if they had to work to open the door, it always snapped shut very quickly. A few times the visitor wouldn't get through before the door closed and they would go away disappointed. Then there were the times the visitor tried to open the door and it wouldn't budge. They would stand and stare at the door, try the knob again, then pound on the door, yelling and begging to be let in. But in these cases, they would always go away dejected and crying incessantly.

All the while I'd stand by, tending my vineyard or olive grove or sometimes roses. There was only one time I wanted to go through the door; the last time I had the dream, as a matter of fact. It was the final time Mata came to visit. This time the door swung wide open and he waltzed through to loud cheers. The light seemed brighter this time and, as the door was closing, I caught a glimpse of Biz on the other side. I dropped my gardening tools and ran to the door, but it closed before I could pass. It was the only time I heard weeping from the other side and it was the only time I suddenly woke up after the dream finished because I was crying also.

After this dream, my depression and grief deepened. My aimless wandering continued, only now I didn't care if I ate or slept or bathed. I thought about returning to the bovine world, but Elsies had lost their appeal and I felt more human than ever; a humanity filled with the old despair that Biz had briefly washed away. Thoughts of ending it all filled my head day and night. I even wandered into Death Valley, a fitting place to end it all. It was July, the temperature was over 110 degrees, and there was no water; only the freedom death would bring.

I started walking right into the heart of that desolate place, commending myself to a God I had shunned and rejected so many times. I walked on and on.

"Why have you done this to me?" I screamed at the clear blue sky. "What is the purpose? Why have you kept me around, made me suffer? I never asked for this; how can you be so cruel?"

I didn't receive an immediate answer, so I kept walking; walking and waiting, but nothing was there but sun and heat and rocks and dried up brush. Farther and farther, aimlessly I shuffled along under the blistering sun. Finally, I gave up. Parched lips, throbbing aching head, and skin baked into a bright red leather gave way to blessed unconsciousness.

It'll be just like in the movies and cartoons, the dried up skull of a cow under the hot desert sky, was my last thought as I lay down on the scorched ground and waited for the freedom that only death could deliver.

God had other ideas.

I woke up in a brightly-lit room surrounded by beeps and tubes and I quickly realized I was in a hospital. For the first time in over three thousand years, I was sick and the people around me had only one concern: my well-being. That was my initial thought, at least.

The nurses displayed nothing but the highest standards of care towards me; however, the doctors saw me as a freak that demanded study rather than therapy. I received proper treatment, I am forced to admit, but in the process, I endured days and days of poking and prodding and needles and probing that left me feeling violated, as if I had been assaulted in a most inappropriate manner.

First there were the medical students; fresh-faced, wearing their short white jackets, pockets bulging with stethoscopes, flashlights, pens, tourniquets, hammers, and anything else that could be used to torment their poor unsuspecting and defenseless patients. I let them gawk for a moment and then abruptly shooed them away.

Then there were the interns and residents, dressed in green scrub suits, mostly looking harried and unkempt with bags under their eyes. Just about every one of these doctors-in-training came through my door with an attitude of combined boredom and frustration. The response upon seeing me was anything but predictable. Some took one look and then turned right around and walked out. Some feigned indifference and did whatever it was they were sent to do, and a few provided me with looks of surprise mixed with fear. These were the honest ones and they were the ones I appreciated the most.

Finally, there was the attending staff, sporting long white coats, gray, white, or no hair, pretending to have an intellectual interest in my "case," while gawking at me as if I were the Abominable Snowman (I actually was once mistaken for good old Abominable, but that's another tale).

I recovered fairly quickly and I think I could have left the hospital after three or four days. But they kept me around.

Each morning I asked the question, "When can I leave?" and invariably, their answer remained, "Soon, in a few days, perhaps." First from Dr. Gotlieb, the ICU doctor with the pointed beard that resembled a loaded pistol. And then, from Dr. Mitchell, the geneticist, who added, "We've still got some test results we're waiting for."

At least he was honest with me.

"You're quite a prize for us here. It's not every day a patient with your unusual manifestations is admitted. Science demands that we study you, your chemical makeup, genetics, physiology, everything. Perhaps what we learn from you will solve some of the great medical mysteries. Cancer, aging, genetic variation, so many things. You must be patient with us and let us learn from you."

His plea softened my heart and I agreed to stay on. And they came and came and came, from all over the globe, to poke and prod and ask me silly questions.

This torture "in the quest for knowledge" went on for several weeks. I had completely recovered from my ordeal in the desert, was up and walking about, and eating whatever I desired; in short I was ready to leave. I paced the lonely halls, flipped through channels on the TV, endured regular visits from "professors" who came to stare, but I was never allowed to leave. There were two security guards posted at the end of my corridor "to keep out unnecessary visitors." All the other rooms were vacant "so we don't alarm the other patients"; once again, I was a prisoner.

There was, however, one visitor I was happy to see. His name was Dr. Klein, Michael to me. He just showed up one morning, standing at the foot of my bed in his green scrubs, staring at me.

"Your horns are longer than I would have guessed," he stated as I looked up at him.

"Your nose is longer than I would have guessed," I replied.

"Do you know why Jews have such big noses?" he asked in his deadpan monotone voice.

"No, tell me," I answered.

"Because the air is free."

I liked him immediately.

"What was it like, living three thousand years ago? Was it better than today? Are the myths about you true?"

I saw a look of desperation on his face; the look of someone who had been searching all his life without an answer, but who now saw the chance to grasp something and hold on to it. Something that had eluded him and would bring him peace if he found it.

"I have a lot more questions to ask. I could fill up an encyclopedia with questions," he added.

"I've been around for a long time and been with some of the most amazing people who've ever lived. Sit down young man and ask your questions," I replied. "What time is it, by the way?"

"It's five thirty in the morning. I've got to leave in thirty minutes to start my rounds. But tell me, in all your years, did you ever see God? I mean, did you ever see Him in person?"

Straight to the point I noticed.

"Now that depends on who your God is. Since you're Jewish (*which I discerned from not only his name, but also his previous joke*), your God would be Jehovah, the God of the Old Testament—er, the Tanach. I never actually saw Him in person, but I was an unfortunate, but lucky, recipient of His wrath."

Dr. Klein looked at his watch again and then replied, "Tell me about it."

"There isn't much to tell. I was in the Sinai desert spying on the Israelites, if you must know, when they saw me and forced me to come down to their camp and be their "god." I didn't have much choice and became caught up in the revelry. They made a golden image of me and brought me their jewels and women—offerings to their new god. Well, this didn't sit well with their true God or with Moses. When Moses finally made his way down from Mt. Sinai, neither he nor God was very happy. Lightning and earthquakes consumed the most heinous offenders. It was all I could do to avoid His wrath. I ended up trapped in a deep crevice, and I would have stayed there if He hadn't deigned to release me."

And I told him the story of the sandstorm and my rescue. He sat mesmerized until I finished; then he looked at his watch, thanked me, and left, promising to return the next day to chat some more.

And he did come back. He was like an eager child who had been kept locked in the dark for years and years, deprived of the most basic of necessities. He asked about everything: good and evil, suffering, joy, elation, but mostly, about God.

"Did you feel any sense of joy at those moments that your life crossed paths with God?" he asked, the yearning in his voice almost palpable.

"Joy? Some I suppose. But more a sense of peace," I answered and then I stared at him. I put my hand to my head and felt the spot that Jesus had touched so many years ago.

"This spot... right here," I continued, pointing to my head. "This is the spot that Jesus touched so many years ago. Afterwards, just looking at it in the mirror gave me a sense of peace. I never understood it until I married Biz. I still don't understand, but I think it's what would be called grace. I saw the violence of God's wrath, completely justified, but, and I'm only realizing this now, I've also been touched by His grace."

At that moment his pager went off and he had to leave.

"I'll see you tomorrow. I want to know more about this 'grace of God.' "

Unfortunately, there wasn't any tomorrow. Shortly afterwards, Armand, that is Dr. Sartori, your college president came to visit. He's the one who rescued me from Death Valley and he is the one responsible for my being here today to chat with you.

Anyway, being as Armand was my "savior," so to speak, he had unrestricted access to my medical prison as well as some authority, as President of a major university. He simply walked in, spoke a few words to my "guards," and we walked out together. He offered me the job of Atwater Chair as Professor of Antiquities and here I am.

This concludes my story. I've covered most of the highlights. I'd like to thank Armand, rather, Dr. Sartori, for all he has done for me. I hope I will see some of you in my class, "Myth and Reality, Separating Fact from Fiction," on Thursdays from seven p.m. until ten p.m.

I have a few minutes to answer some questions, but there is also a reception that will start at six o'clock in the meeting room across the hall. I hope to see all of you there.

Now, if the ushers can escort those with questions to the microphones.

At that moment there was a flash of light, followed by a popping noise, and then a second flash and pop. The Minotaur slumped to the ground as blood began to pour from his neck and chest. Chaos followed as President Sartori rushed to his side, while others seemed more intent on gathering samples of his blood. President Sartori cradled the dying Minotaur in his arms.

There was a look of peace in the fallen beast's eyes as he whispered:

"Finally free... the door... the Light... Biz."
An unmistakable smile appeared on his face.

And he died.

About the Author

David Gelber, a New York native, is the seventh of nine sons and one of three to pursue medicine. He graduated from Johns Hopkins University in 1980 and went on to graduate medical school in 1984 from the University of Rochester.

He completed his residency at Baylor University Medical Center in Dallas, Texas, followed by three years as attending surgeon at Nassau County Medical Center in Long Island, N.Y. Gelber has since joined Coastal Surgical Group in Houston, Texas.

Gelber has been a surgeon for more than 20 years, but over the last few years he began to pursue his passion for writing, initially with his debut novel, *Future Hope* (Emerald Book Company, January 2010). The novel speculates about future Earth and what the world might have been like if man had not succumbed to temptation in the Garden of Eden. *Joshua and Aaron* is a sequel to *Future Hope* and follows the battle of wills that transpires between unsung hero Joshua Smith and satanic Aaron Diblonski.

Dr. Gelber has added two books about surgery, *Behind the Mask* and *Under the Drapes,* both of which provide the reader with a view of the world of surgery rarely seen by those outside the medical professions.

Last Light is an apocalyptic short story which starts off asking the question: "What would happen if nobody ever was sick or injured?"

Minotaur Revisited is an entertaining romp through history seen through the eyes of Quint, the famed half-bull half-man monster of Greek Mythology.

Gelber was raised in reformed Judaism, but joined the Presbyterian Church 15 years ago. He is married with three children, four dogs, and a variety of birds. His interests include horse racing, mechanical Swiss watches and, of course, writing.

www.ingramcontent.com/pod-product-compliance
Lightning Source LLC
Chambersburg PA
CBHW020758250626
47155CB00003B/1129